WHEN EVERYTHING WAS POSSIBLE

When Everything Was Possible

Greg Bernhardt

Haybine Press
Salisbury, Vermont

When Everything Was Possible
First Edition, December 2016

Published in the United States by Haybine Press
80 Goats, Inc., 2001 Old Jerusalem Road, Salisbury, VT 05769.
Printed in the United States of America.

The text of this publication was set in ITC Garamond.

ISBN: 978-0-9983524-4-2

Library of Congress Control Number: 2016919273

for my wife
Hannah Sessions

Acknowledgements

For his editorial advice, encouragement and friendship, I want to thank Edouard Collet.

For her honest and creative perspective, loving support and inspiration, I want to thank Hannah Sessions.

For Livia and Hayden, I want to thank you both for your support, but most of all for your kindness and optimism.

Poetry comes nearer to vital truth than history.

—Plato

On the Trail

Sunlight breaks through the trees as she picks up her belongings, adjusts her socks in her shoes, and sets off again along the trail. Her spirits attune to the change in weather. The rocks on the path dry quickly in the heat. There will be few memories of the rains by the end of the day, only the tree roots sucking up the water in the topsoil will remember.

I see my young body move through these hills, pass over the ridges of these mountains, years ago. In another life, perhaps some other body too. It's unclear. I was her, wandering in the distance there. I see her move, her fit legs taking strides one after the other, strong and deliberate to hike another fifteen miles that day. Conversing only with her watch, more intuitively than mathematically, she adjusts her pace. I know approximately what day it is. I know her trail name. I know her like a twin sister, yet she sees me only in daydreams of another life.

She crosses a stream, which was not a stream five days ago. Having only one pair of shoes, she takes care with each step. The trail is rocky and, where there are no rocks, it is mud. Bird calls are the only sounds other than her footsteps, but only now, hours since daybreak, does she notice. Insects teem. The flies bother her. She rubs oil over her arms and neck, pats her cheeks and forehead, and then runs her hands through her short blonde hair. Sweat coats her skin and mixes with the essential oils, brewing a smell that she breathes in with pleasure. The sky is ultramarine blue. The sun is full and hot. There is no wind today, and she looks forward to reaching the ridgeline. There will be a view and a clearing where she can sit and feel the rare calm at the top. It will be dry there by the time she arrives.

Hours pass in silence. She stops, looking left and right. Like an animal in the wood, she is unaware of herself. She moves through the trees as if they were her habitat, where she was born and would die, familiar with everything. She looks outward without thoughts or feelings, only moving. Eyes see rocks. Legs lift. The course is determined already. Up she climbs. Hands grab a tree and pull the body upward. Does she know where she is? The body keeps moving as the heart keeps pumping, the lungs keep breathing, and the eyes keep sensing. She is unconscious of herself being human. A sound. The crack of wood below her feet, beneath the leafy mess of the trail, or something else, she doesn't know. She wakes back to the moment and sees birds fly off, startled by her presence. She is reminded that she is an outsider. She sees her feet wearing hiking shoes and her bare knees. She sees her yellow shorts, her naked stomach and purple sports bra. Aware again. She observes from the mind's eye and marvels at how it was that she drifted away from herself like that. Who was making those decisions? Walking, turning, advancing forward and upward. She is conscious of her self now, the image of her whole body as she hikes along. A tall lean figure, exposed skin tanned by weeks outdoors, hair bleached by the sun and washed only by streams and rivers. Muscles youthful and firm. She tightens her jaw and sees her face, her beautifully serious face, contradicted by her smile. She is ever childlike, a ten-year-old in spirit.

The mountain's trees shade her, their leaves full grown and dark green. But no more beech and maple, at this elevation it is mostly spruce and pine and other coniferous trees, and they grow smaller as she ascends. The tens of thousands, the millions of trees that have enclosed her for weeks now, shield her from seeing beyond where she is. She spends the mass of hours protected from the world outside of this immediate tapestry of green, this short radius of earth. The time spent there and this place itself have protected her. General relativity applies to her in the universe of inward perspective. She uses this small space, the changing trees, rocks, and trails that guide her, as barriers from all else beyond. She tracks the solitude, which is amicably ahead of her right now.

The sun, which is not in the sky, but in the air around her. It's light is born just beyond the treetops, travels over her like a breeze. She is the only one in this world. She's not seen anyone since before the rains. Her isolation has reached a pinnacle, but carrying her on is the knowledge of the ridgeline, the clearing above, the rocky meadow where everything will turn upside down. Black will become white, shade will lift to exposure, the stillness will subside to a flow of air, and the introversion of her soul will open across the enormity of a new expansive world. Individual trees will be replaced with a shade of color along hill tops, and she once again will see a world that right now is far away from her. She will feel the weight of how small she is and unleash the weight of how big she was.

Others are there when she arrives. Two boys with their backs to her look outward as she approaches the steep rock face. Another one is off to the right. He rests too. That one alone. She stops only seconds after discovering them all there. Standing motionless, she forgets who or what she is. She is an animal surprised by human activity, but her mind registers it all and realizes that she too is one of them. She too is a human being. She wipes the sweat from her forehead and sides of her nose.

As is typical for her upon first cresting the top of a mountain, she says nothing to anyone, and no one attempts to acknowledge her just yet. She finds a spot, sits, adjusts herself. She takes off her baseball cap and runs her hands through the sweat on her scalp, shifting hair off her forehead so that the sun may rain down on her face. She closes her eyes and breathes, as if in a religious observance. Then she opens and looks. A smile appears in her eyes. A small one, just to herself, for humor, and all its insights, is a forgotten skill one sometimes loses while alone for so long.

She is now. I am there. I always can go back to those spots on a mountain's clearing.

It is not long before she starts to register the muffled sounds of the others and begins to comprehend what they are saying as specific words. Her self-imposed deafness lifts, and she hears them now with full clarity.

I listen to the two boys sitting beside the mountain's steepest edge. They laugh and talk loud enough for her to hear. In these hills, such cliff-like ledges are an uncommon sight, so they often are visited for their sublime perspective. This one in particular is dramatic enough for them to discuss the obvious dangers of sitting so close to it. People who venture to this look-out with dogs or small children would surely keep far from the precipice. But for two twenty-something men, this is what they have been pursuing through these trees and up these winding inclines. They laugh like young boys, heedless and over-confident, but they don't push or shove at each other like young boys might. As she follows their conversation, she discerns that, despite its joking nature, it is laden with allusions to the more introspective thoughts of philosophers from old books rather than the superficial currents of recent culture. One of them makes casual note of something often discussed by those who find themselves by steep mountain rocks: the queerness of feeling quite a bit uneasy, but not due to the possibility of accidentally falling over the edge.

I know what you're talking about.

I can't remember... I think it was Sartre who said that it isn't so much being afraid of falling, but instead being aware that all humans possess the knowledge that they have free will to decide to "throw themselves over"... if they choose.

Do you think he came up with that sitting on a cliff?

Probably. Most great thoughts, I would assume, come from people who sat on the tops of mountains.

In my religion class a couple of years ago, we talked about this in regard to Kierkegaard. He saw it as coming from man's growing sense of anxiety in the modern world. Man used to be concerned only with fear, that is, being afraid of things. A wolf, a bear, an enemy, starvation, falling. But anxiety is different. Anxiety is man's staring into "the abyss" and feeling angst. In being free, man has a choice, and it is the choice that gives him anxiety.

Yeh, survival does seem easier in some ways, doesn't it? Trying to avoid falling, rather than sitting safely here, wondering about all this shit.

There is something familiar about the two boys sitting in the quiet sun atop this mountain, talking about things they had learned in college. She recognizes them as similar to others she had known. They are not entirely foolish, she decides, by sitting so close to the edge. What really is the difference from where they are and from where she had placed herself? Not to mention the boy who was sitting alone with his back to them all. It's not like they are dangling their legs over the edge or standing right at the last bits of rock. Perhaps they got just close enough?

I reach into my backpack and get some water. I drink a good deal of it and break off some chocolate, just a pinch, as my reward, my communion. The two boys look at me now, noticing my ritual has concluded and has become an everyday task. I can be interrupted, they decide. The one with long hair speaks to me first.

Which direction did you come from?

I'm heading North. Which way are you going?

North too.

Then the other one speaks.

We saw a light through the trees the other night. During the storm. Was that you?

I don't know. Maybe.

Well, the guy sitting over there—he was set up south of us, quite a ways back, so we know it wasn't him.

She had been alone out there, she had believed. Seen nothing. Heard nothing. The idea they were present after-all begins to sink into her, shattering illusions about her time in the storms.

I didn't see anyone else.

How long have you been out here?

A couple of weeks or so. How 'bout you?

We got started six days ago. The first day was perfect. The forecast said it would only rain our second day out, but then... We didn't intend on covering so little ground in our first week.

How far are you going?

I don't know, now that we got set back a few days. We have two more weeks before we gotta go back.

How far do you think you will go?

I don't know. At first I thought I would go all the way to Katahdin. But over the last week, my expectations have changed.

The rain you mean?

Probably. I just don't worry about where I want to get to in the end.

Where are you from?

No one had asked me that since starting into the woods. At this stage in my young life, I don't feel I am from anywhere just yet. My younger self was from somewhere. My older self would be from somewhere. But my fresh young adult mind and body is all right there in the woods, on the ridgeline, with and within my backpack and the moveable home that is my tent.

Here. The Northeast.

Yeh, we're from outside of Boston. We went to college here though.

He rubs his mouth with his hands.

Listen, we're going to camp at the lean-to just before the summit here. We asked the guy over there if he wanted to make camp together tonight. If you want to join us, there's room for all of us there.

I'm not sure if I'll keep going this afternoon or not. I'll see. Thanks though.

They leave me alone then. We say it was nice meeting each other, and they go back to their spot on the ridgeline. The other boy sitting alone still has not turned his head in my direction, and he remains a curiosity to me as I sit drinking water and snacking on nuts. I don't admit it with my gestures or the way I look at any of the boys there on the mountain, but I sit with the secret of having really enjoyed seeing others and, what's more, their light flirtations. The truth is I feel like they are the only people in the world right now, and joining them for the night seems like the right thing to do. I hadn't laughed in days, maybe even weeks. I can't remember. Hearing others' voices already feels like a gift. I appreciate them and am drawn to them, as if it is an instinct to be drawn to my own species, as if my very survival depends on it. I want to see the boy with the longish hair smile at me again. I want to be around the energy of the other boy with him. His enthusiasm reminds me of the bigger world out beyond these woods, of towns, teeming cities, and the great populations that are out there somewhere. I want the other boy on the precipice to turn around so I can see his face. Who is he? And why is he alone? Would he meet up with the other boys at the lean-to tonight?

The light from the sun blankets the ridgeline without an obstructing cloud to dampen its effects on all of us. The weather has settled now and hints that it would remain so for the following week at the least.

While hiking, the contemplative side of my nature rises to the surface, and I employ the greater length of my waking hours with resting my thoughts on things, letting them linger there to ferment into something yet undiscovered, or yet understood.

The young woman who is walking these trails now, urging herself through the world of trees and mountain, wrapped up in the natural world, ruminates aimlessly about like a deer chewing at the bark of a tree, then some leaves, then a fern plant, some wide leafy green weed, dried up twig meat and so on. The physical world is no longer external, but mirrors her inward reflections. Even crossing paths with others doesn't disrupt her musings, and the others transform from characters into passing ideas.

Hello.

Hello.

They smile as they pass, but mostly she looks in their eyes to get a sense about them. Where did they come from? Then they disappear into the labyrinth of vegetation.

Even as the rain falls and she struggles to make a simple meal, when a blister forms on her ankle, or when the bugs begin to pester her with such relentlessness, she sustains a general perspective of contemplation. It is her habit now.

She approaches a place that looks right for a tent. It is protected and has the feel of having been settled by other hikers. She comes to a stop and discovers some rocks gathered in a circle, a clear fire site. Nothing else but a clearing enough for two small tents. She lets down her pack and starts on her routine. First her tent. Some unpacking of things. Setting up her bed, sleeping bag with an insulated foam mattress underneath. Laying out her sleeping clothes. Then food prep. Rice tonight with some dried fruit, but first she looks for a water source. She presumes one might be nearby, since others had settled here previously. She prepares a place about thirty yards away as a latrine for later. Starts a fire where the rocks are arranged with some small sticks and dried leaves that lie everywhere as her fuel. She takes an iodine tablet diluted in her water as if it were her daily vitamin or medication and feels humbled, conceding her obvious vulnerability in contrast to all other animal life thriving around her. She is a foreigner, she is reminded, a visitor in her own world.

The ritual of eating alone outdoors differs in countless ways from the habits of preparing and consuming food in a house or a restaurant. The mark of real divergence for her is what she does as she eats her dinner. Instead of looking over to someone else's face, exchanging words about the day or what will come tomorrow. Instead of people watching from an outdoor café on some city street, she looks around at the landscape and finds herself enveloped in the evening. She takes note of what lays about the forest floor, the stage of decay of fallen tree limbs, the size and color of rocks, any changes in plant life. Smells the air. Peers up through the thick green mass of leaves to a departing light in the sky. Listens to the chiming of insect life, one of many distinct sounds that emerge. She pays attention to the temperature outside as it cools and to the nuances of this transition, trying to decide if any of it means anything.

After finishing her meal and cleaning up, she begins her final activity before retiring into her tent. She assembles some found sticks, small stones, and other things that lie on the forest floor. By the side of a thick tree, she sets six small twigs into the dirt, finds some lengths of flexible pine branches and ties them from one twig to another, leading them to the center of a tenuous shape. In between the pebbles, she places some wide green leaves in spiral patterns with a small rock stationed atop each to hold them from any winds that might come along. The whole sculpture is only about eight inches in diameter and rises off the surface of the ground ten inches at its highest point. Each night the structure alters in shape and form. The archetypes resemble each other, but overall each one is unique and derived from the objects found that night. The size is relatively the same each time, but she makes sure they are out of the way of paths, sometimes even invisible to the trail. Always by the side of large trees and always with the care of an artist, she creates an installation in a place she will never see again. She records its final look only in her memory and knows they will last only a couple of days, maybe a week or even a month depending on the weather. Anyway, it doesn't matter much.

She does not fully understand the purpose of this activity. It is an act of instinct, serving its purpose in the way that sculpting the sands on the shores of the ocean satisfies a child. She continues to sift the loose earth, running her hand over top to smooth out the holes and bumps and raking off all the putrefying debris. She frames the image with a border of dirt and woody scraps. She is not interested in the permanency of the thing, recognition, or what it is even. It is as fleeting as the reds and oranges in the lower western sky and as significant to the beholder. After some time just looking, she goes into her tent.

I see my body there as I change my clothes. A smoothness runs along all of me. I am not aware of how beautiful I am. But I am not ashamed of myself either. I have built up a security with my nakedness, something new to me and unknown until the past weeks here alone in the woods. I can see my body for what it is. I see my shape. My particular features. My calf muscles have been an attribute I always admired. Now I appreciate even my somewhat round tummy and hips that renovated me into a woman without my consent. The contours of my breasts and their slope, I forget to think about defining this part of myself. The preoccupation is gone in this moment, and I walk out of my tent to stand alone in the wood as the light wanes. All of me. I transition not into a nudist, but a human without inhibition or exhibition. Only for the moment though, I am certain of it.

After stretching in the cool of the night, I crawl back into my tent and slip into my sleeping clothes. My eyes dilate and adjust to the night. I close them and try to fall asleep. No thoughts. Only feelings left undescribed and images painted brightly in my head, intersecting with the awakening unconscious.

Her traveler's dreams partly propel her travel. An excited trepidation arises. Not knowing what will occur next and taking in the newness of things heightens her sense of being alive. Time slows to the rate at which a child experiences the world, and her dreams reach rarified levels of intensity and arousal from the exploration of foreign places.

She is anxious to exit her tent in the morning, since her breath has formed a humid cloud inside. The odor of vinyl encased with dew has settled in the tent as well. But the air outside cools her lungs and dries the sleep off of her face. During the morning, she thinks more lightly and allows herself to smile. Her eyes are lit with the prospects of the adventure of a new day. She easily makes breakfast, brews coffee, and packs up without thinking it work or a chore. Only a few tasks must be completed each day, and, during most of the time, she may be idle if she desires. So when work must be done, she readily accepts it. She looks forward to it even and enjoys the necessity of its purpose. She must pack and unpack her belongings several times a day. It is a conversation with herself when she does it. Material possessions on the trail mean more to her than they might normally otherwise. It is all she has with which she may identify herself. Everyday items must prove useful and worth the weight on her back; she takes pride in her strength and the hardened muscles throughout her back.

When she has just about finished cleaning and packing up, a stranger emerges from the trail to the south of her. She first hears him, humming a quiet tune to himself. Not a song. Just sounds, nothing harmonious. Then she spots his form in the distance and notices a red bandana tied around his neck. The boy that had been sitting on the ridge alone. She adjusts her hair and smooths the skin around her cheeks with one hand. She doesn't know why she is nervous. Many times people have crossed paths with her. Ascending, descending, stepping off to the side to let her pass. On occasion, someone will be resting on a boulder somewhere, taking water and a quick breath. She might stop even, say something. Ask some questions. Respond jovially. There on the mountain top she had conversed with others, even saw this very boy sitting fifteen yards away, for over an hour. But now is a new scenario playing out. It is early, before day hikers even get started. They are far down the trail, away from any summits or peaks. The trail feels more like a private walkway at this early hour, the yard in front of her home. Someone is approaching her property. Her space. Now is not for the public highways of the mountain.

As the tall figure nears her, she takes note of his dark and tangled hair, wavy from weeks on the trail and tucked back behind his ears. It is not long, it could be just enough to reach the sides of his jaw bone. When he reaches her, he stops and looks to her as if they know each other.

Good morning.

Good morning.

She faces her reflection, a different version of herself, imagined out of the thick woods of her mind, conjured up from a stray thought that had escaped the internal world, manifested now right here before her in physical form. They stand together on the trail head as if this had been their meeting place, decided upon weeks previous. Here they are now, right on time, where they had planned to be.

Travelers are the most elusive characters to assess. It has been said that a traveler is inclined to misfortune, even after having been cared for by so many serendipitous strangers and events. In the end, it is opportune for him to put an end to his wanderings, to resolve some motive to cease. A traveler, she knows, is much more likely to harbor some secret, a reason why he moves away from where he was. He could be anyone. There is little to go on, nothing with much telling to it. And from his perspective, you may be just another view, like the one stretched out before the tourist from a mountain top village. Something to take in briefly before departing for the next sight.

She notices his posture and reads him to be an unlikely traveler. He is new at it, like her, and there is an open quality about his features, something naïve almost. They glance at the trail in both directions, up at the sky and down to the ground, then back to one another's gaze. Unlike other moments of crossing paths with strangers, they are not crossing paths. Their paths are meeting up at the same point, and their projected route is one and the same. She is not resting. He is not heading in the opposite direction. This is not a public clearing. They are both stepping out in the same way, and this is evident to both in their reasoning of the situation.

Did you see the sunrise this morning?

Yes. It was wonderful.

Did you camp here last night?

Asking the questions aloud that have been answered already in our thoughts.

Yes.

Are you heading out right now?

I was about to.

Neither one of us asks the question that we both don't know the answer to.

We talk until his motions reveal that he is going to restart his journey. I make some last minute adjustments to my shoes and socks and begin walking along side of him. Perhaps I will walk a bit with him as we finish our exchange. But that is uncertain. We will not completely digest the strangeness of our meeting until the journey is over. Right now, for both of us, it is unclear when that will be.

Have you noticed the water tastes better around here?

I think it is because the rains have stopped. Don't you think?

Yeah. I was trying my best to gather rain to drink from those large plant leaves, the ones about ten inches wide and a foot and half or so long. It was good.

Do you have any left?

A little. Do you want to try some?

She hesitates. She was about to say maybe later when we stop, but she did not know how far they would keep walking together. She wanted to say no also, I can't take the last of your rain water. But he offered.

Sure.

It's good isn't it?

Yes. Thank you.

Sharing a drink proves easy for them. The act also tells her that she will continue on with him for a while.

Did you camp with those two guys from the ridgeline yesterday?

No.

Did they invite you too?

Yes.

It seems to occur to him after some time of walking together that he should tell her his name. Gabe. I'm Anna. Once a name is attributed to the tall figure to her right, he becomes more solid and recognizable as someone born not just from her imagination. He is a veritable person with a past history, even beyond the precipice of that rock face where she had first spotted him. They do not speak about the previous weeks or of any point in time stretching backwards. They focus on the present with vague allusions to some points in the future. He comments about the sunlight that scatters across the ferny meadow beneath the trees. She talks about her tendencies to constantly look for tracks left by animals. She keeps a log in her journal, makes a quick sketch from memory of the track and gives a guess at what it could be. She usually does this at midday when she eats her lunch, scribbles things down that she has observed. She does not offer to the pages monologues about her thoughts or anything from her mental landscape. Only the momentary facets of things that she witnesses in the physical world document her journey.

The custom is new to this time in her life. She keeps the record, not for herself now, but for the sake of someone years from now, unknown to her, maybe her older self or a future child. The thoughts that survive the rummaging and discarding along the dirt trail are for her alone, in this instant. They are unimportant to the future and will be forgotten. What she sees in the mountain landscape, small and large observations of the ordinary and the sublime, she captures in quick sketches and fragment sentences that seem more scientific than artistic. Rendering the details of a fern, the texture of a tree's bark, the slope of a hill. Mapping out what she sees, she is making a journal that will allow the reader to accompany her along the actual trail. Her ability to detach herself from her ego and simply observe, plotting the course in lines that never allude to an interior world of her own, that mirrors the trail itself, how the rock steps and the bending way around this or that express the instinctual design of its creators. In the end, neither the way of her words nor the way of the trail itself distract the story that is told.

There is so much contradiction out here.

What do you mean?

She doesn't elaborate any further. She says she doesn't know why and leaves it at that.

I think there is always contradiction in everything we do and see.

She agrees with him for the most part.

She can tell that Gabe is troubled by something. A girl, she guesses, but that is not the reason he is out here. She discerns this not because of any real sadness that he conveys, he shows none. His whole attitude is upbeat and light. Her analysis focuses on his trace disinterest in her as a creature worthy of flirtation. This persists through the end of the day, when it is time to camp and they still have not parted ways. There will be no chance for splitting up at this point. The light fades fast, and they remain together. He sets his tent up as far from her as he can without making an obvious decision that they should have different settlements. They will share a fire and even cook together, but when it comes time for sleep, a line has been drawn by the placement of his shelter. It could be for any reason, but other details she has noted during their hike point to a withdrawn demeanor and guarded heart. Nothing crying out for pity. Nothing dark. Perhaps it is her female intuition that has her notice any of this. He has tried, over the course of getting to know her, to hide all of him from her, wishing only to share in the present with her.

Gabe becomes terse around the matter of food preparation and his need for a fresh water source. Unusual for a hiker or outdoorsperson. He shows a child's pickiness in choosing from what part of a river he will take water. Having investigated all likely contamination possibilities, he convinces himself the water is good here. It is cold he says. I need cold water. The lack of peanut butter in his pack is what baffles her most. He likes it, but not as a staple in his diet. He has found every occasion to digress off the trail when possible and seek to procure fresh breads and expensive cured meats, local artisanal cheeses from the farms that produce them. He makes sure always to have a bit of wine in a glass bottle for evening meals and creates an altogether fancy array of delights around the occasion of the evening meal. He cooks warm meals whenever possible, he tells her. Less chance of getting sick while out here. That is what he tells her, but it is clear he wants it that way. His oddities place him outside of hiking culture, and he doesn't seem very aware that there is such a thing. This and his humility charm her, as if observing the customs of a foreigner. She finds his quirky seriousness about the simple things in life to be intriguing rather than an annoyance.

One afternoon a few days later, on a heavily visited part of the trail, they meet a day hiker. This one they talk with for some time. His story interests her and Gabe. Amidst the sea of travelers they have come across, he is dressed in the most distinguished manner. He wears black pants, seemingly pressed, like ones worn for work or a semi-formal party. His shirt is colored with thick horizontal stripes and tucked in. A slick, shiny black belt holds him to a certain standard, not quite preppie, more urban. He is young, but older than they are. Maybe thirty. He is short and dark skinned with well-groomed hair and a smooth face. Anyone clean-shaven is a dead give-away to be a day hiker, and the lack of any pack makes this even more certain about him. He walks quickly up to the point where they are. He stops, looks about, and then moves to another vantage point. He repeats this again and again in different places within yards of one another.

Here, gaps in the trees give only glimpses of some of the valley below. It is clear that they are close to the top, but something about this spot gives people the inclination to pause before the final ascent. The atmosphere is more social than at the top, where people usually keep more to themselves, humbled by the breathtaking views.

He speaks a word aloud. Anna hears it but does not understand. He had said it to himself in the direction of the valley floor, an utterance he seemed unable to resist as he peered out beyond the branches. He stands with his arms at his sides without any pretense in his posture. Anna is close to him yet unnoticed. Perhaps, he would not have ever registered her as a fellow person sharing this space if she had not spoken. She doesn't do so right away. Fifteen seconds go by before she reacts to his curious word. It is unlike her to ask something of anyone along the trail, especially one privately exploring nature or in a reflective moment. The way he spoke felt so intimate, though, that she couldn't hold back. By chance or not, she had been close enough to his ground to be part of his experience. Whether he liked it or not and whether she liked it or not.

What was that? What you said?

He cocks his head toward her, as if unsure whether the voice to his right is directed at him or to someone else. He becomes aware of her proximity and catches her gaze in his periphery. He completes the rotation of his neck and meets her full on.

Pardon?

The word? The word you just said? While looking down below.

He is a bit taken aback by her boldness. He smiles widely, showing all of his teeth. It seems to be his way of reacting to anything he doesn't fully understand. His smile makes the discomfort of the situation dissolve. It disarms her, and she is certain it could for whomever he regards.

I was speaking a word in my language.

He pauses.

The name of where I was born.

She had been preparing herself for a different response. She had imagined that he had uttered something in his language used to describe something beautiful or tremendous. Perhaps something that could be used casually with a stranger like "isn't it wonderful" or "what a perfect day." She had begun something though and couldn't leave it at that, despite feeling conflicted at prying anymore than she already had. It is unusual for her to get herself into a predicament such as this, and Gabe listens from a short distance. He is far enough away not to get involved at first. He is not in a position to help her out, but the man's smile continues to draw her in nevertheless.

Why? Where were you born?

I am from Rwanda. The region I am from looks just like this. Since I left, I have not been to a place, until now, which looks so much like my home.

Really? This looks like Rwanda?

Yes.

He looks at Anna again and smiles so fully that a laugh emerges. Gesturing and more conscious of himself now, he begins to describe the similarities with the valley below, even the mountain upon which they stand. His English is good, but the novelty of his accent resounds to the ears of both her and Gabe. She notices a strange scar stretching at least six to seven inches down his left forearm. Three thick lines, like the mark of animal's thrashing. It is so prominent, and his skin seems so traumatized by whatever caused this. She can't stop staring at it every time he points at things in the distance.

You see there. That green color. And the shape of those fields.

After some time listening to the man, Gabe moves closer. Smiling widely, he asks the man questions about where he lives now.

I live forty minutes north of here.

And you haven't seen any of these views before?

I work and have not left to go anywhere since I arrived. A woman I work with, she told me I should take a day off and do something. For myself. She lent me her car to go somewhere outside the city. She said the best thing to do in this state is hike or swim. I don't swim, so

I came here.

So there are hiking trails in Rwanda like this?

Not like this, no.

He laughs and explains that he never before has been on a hike for recreation.

He laughs and smiles even more, which seems impossible, until his smile truly does cover all of his face. It is contagious. He marvels at the journey Anna is on and that she and Gabe met only recently out here in the woods, wandering along these trails. He doesn't ask why they do what they are doing. He doesn't question the motivations for such activity; it seems to occur to him as incidental, like why someone chooses a certain dwelling, in one place or another. He registers their circumstances for what they are and that alone: this young woman and this young man are both, at that moment, walking and camping in these woods.

Anna glances at his black pants and wonders if he is hot. He is the only one wearing pants, and sweat is pouring off everyone's faces this afternoon.

Would you like any water? It's really hot today.

No. Thank you.

I've got plenty, are you sure... Please, have some.

Once she insists, he has to accept. It is his upbringing perhaps, to acquiesce once somebody offers you something three times. He takes a small amount and thanks her. His large smile disappears momentarily, and he gives her a humble nod and gracious gaze. His whole persona is foreign to her, but not in a way that is obvious at first. It is only well into their conversation that she begins to discern the nuances in his mannerisms, the signals that he is from a different culture. They are attractive to both her and Gabe, and she unknowingly begins to mimic them subtly in their conversation. If she could look closely at herself in a mirror, she would see that her smile stretches to previously unknown dimensions, shaping her jawline and cheekbones in a new way.

And where are you from? What country?

She is a bit confused. Perhaps he used the wrong word, getting a bit off in his English. But she decides it would be polite to answer his question the way it is stated.

Here.

No, really? You have an accent, don't you?

She's startled. People often ask her where in the country she has lived, not being quite able to place the interesting way she speaks. She has a slow and deliberate pronunciation, one perhaps developed in trying to correct some early childhood impediment and having led to a sort of poetic deliverance of her sounds. It has people listen to her. It gives thoughtfulness to whatever it is she has to say. That uncommon quality makes her seem as coming from somewhere else.

But how... You can hear an accent in English?

Yes. I grew up speaking English. More and more as I got older.

I'm sorry. I don't know what language people speak in Rwanda. I would have guessed French more than English.

Yes. That too.

Anna wants to ask him more questions and learn about why he is here, why he left Rwanda, what he does for work. But she knows there are refugee populations in many small New England cities, and she doesn't feel it appropriate to ask. The scar on his arm makes her hesitation grow to the point where she falters in asking him anything about his life. Gabe doesn't shy away though. She thinks that maybe he hasn't seen the man's scar from where he is sitting and that maybe he doesn't know the man is probably a refugee. Maybe it doesn't matter to Gabe.

What do you do for work?

I work in a market. It sells food to Rwandans mainly.

Do you like it here?

That question seems too personal, and Anna cringes a little when Gabe asks it. She wonders why she does. It is her fault for even intruding in the first place. Before she can worry anymore about making this man uncomfortable, he flashes a smile and offers them a glimpse of his bright eyes, answering that without a doubt he does in fact like it very much. With another laugh, he puts out his palm in the direction of the valley below and says the word again, which she still fails to record in her memory. He speaks the name of his home and reiterates to her that this looks just like Rwanda. And then, as if he knows that Anna is feeling trepidation about Gabe's question, the man changes the direction of their conversation.

The water. That water... it just occurred to me how different it tasted.

Oh... I'm sorry, I forgot to mention there is a bit of iodine in the water, but it is barely noticeable. It's lake water. But it is safe, I assure you.

That is it. It tastes like water I drank back in Rwanda. We used the same treatment in our water.

At this point, with familiarities reaching such strange heights, they begin to resemble old friends being reunited. They sit together and talk more about what else there is to see in the area. They learn his name. Kurembera. He tells them more about his home, and Anna begins to feel as if they have been transported there. For brief instants, she can see in his face that he is talking to them as if he is their guide to knowing all there is to discover. With nothing in sight to distinguish this land from his, with no towns or cities in the distance, it just as well could be any place on earth where the rains come and the sun shines, where the fields are farmed and ancient mountains still hold some ground. Anna realizes that this place through which she has been walking is not hers alone to see or Gabe's. It is as much Kurembera's. Seeing this makes the moment richer, more succinct and less so at the same time. Again her bearing shifts slightly, and all the ideas she has compressed into her person are affected. Even with defensive guards up, she allows her young adult mind to take in the world around her, the people, all of it, sending beacons of wonder. My older mind can reconnect with the power of this unity if I remember to allow my young self to be my mother, my first example.

Evening comes to the mountain. Kurembera has left, and all the crowds are gone. She asks Gabe if he sees any of this too, if he can hear the message underlying what is transpiring at any given moment, if the events around him offer him the same feeling. As she shares her thoughts of the day, Gabe is challenged to stop filtering the universe through a self-centered view of his role in it. A door is opened slightly. She can see that Gabe, despite being outdoors all this time, is just beginning to get a true glimpse of the expansiveness of the world around him. It is clear to her that, for whatever reason, Gabe has been surrounded by four walls this whole time, perhaps his whole life. His naïve nature attracts her nevertheless. The two of them stare at the branches swaying in the darkness above. There are no stars to observe, but the sky seems limitless that night. Resting alone together on the side of that mountain, they imagine a place similar to this one, a valley just like this one, a world with myriad images of itself, reflecting in all directions.

For a week now the two travelers have hiked a stretch of the Green Mountain National Forest, traversing eighty miles. The sun still reigns over this whole swath of New England. Each clearing they pass through offers a diaphanous blue sky and tender breezes that sweep over the mountain peaks. The entire universe of these woods assumes an especially dreamlike quality. The trail seems to take shape as they approach, rocks shift and sculpt their pathway. The trees shed sunlight there and now here, illuminating the quiet hum of the wild in a serene and biddable light. It could be that providence is laying a hand in it all. Or their perspectives have been revised.

Gabe leans back on a rock. It is the middle of the day, and they rest while it is hottest. Despite the heat, he does not forgo the chance to flood himself with sunlight, as the trail almost always gives shade to them. The opportunity must be taken.

His shirt is off, his red bandana and his hat. The boyish attributes of his physique mingle with the aspects of a man coming forth in his widening shoulders and the definitive sprouting of hair along the center of his chest. She sees his adult self ripening in his naked torso, stirring a new kind of attraction in herself, a foreign desire for something more intimate and primal. She is not completely aware of all this exactly. Her reflections do not reveal any of this to her consciously. What she does notice is that she wants to get a good look at him as he shuts his eyes for a moment.

Her own body is also somewhat bare for him to discern. Unlike the dark olive which permeates his tanned skin, a warm blush underlies her tan stomach, shoulders, legs and arms. Her blue sports bra delineates many details of her body. She is often shy about her shape and what it means to a boy. It's been evident from the start that something in Gabe checks any attempts to delight in viewing her body. It would not be until later the next day, when the two of them reach a lake hidden atop these mountains, that they would both strip down to their underwear to swim there in seclusion. Then it would be forced upon him to look at her and make some opinion in his mind. This moment presents no test however. A shield still stands between him and the rest of the world, including her. Maybe he could see her as an idea running to the water, but he does not betray the signs of one imagining the true shape and color of what is concealed. His eyes do not sneak at her, and she wonders why. Almost out of frustration, she secretly thinks that she might just take off all of her clothing, just to see how he might react. While swimming, she would consider unclothing completely and swimming over to the other side of the lake. Pretend to find a private space to lay naked in the sun for moment, all the while knowing he would continue to be a part of her scene and have access to see her. Any residual shyness would be subdued by the distance at which he would be able observe her body. Any particulars over which she still suffers insecurity would be softened in the final image presented to him from afar.

She does not do it though.

The relationship between them was born without their approval or intentions and is taking shape without their guiding its formation. Theirs is a communing of two persons not dissimilar to that of two deer finding one another in an otherwise deerless environment and continuing together for no reason other than their commonality. There is no need in it. Neither came to find the other. He never released any musky deer odor in hopes of attracting a female, and she never sniffed the air for his scent. The thought occurs to her time and time again that he simply may pick up and go on his own way, without more than a so long, and not notice a difference the next day. He would not miss her company. He would not need to see her again, or anyone in particular. He is not guarding himself from her out of a sadness, she decides. He is this way. He is unlike the other deer in the wood.

What do you daydream about out here?

You mean, what do I think about? I feel as though all my thoughts are daydreams.

No, I don't think that's true. I have noticed a difference in my thinking here. There are times when I am very clearly reflecting on past events, actual things that have happened. Then there is a practical side reflecting on the things I can see with my own two eyes, what is right in front of me now. Finally, even, the realistic dreams of what lies ahead in my future, once I am done out here. But what I mean is, what are the dreamlike thoughts that come to the surface? Do you imagine yourself living like this forever? Do you wonder ever how you would survive as an animal out here, like a bird or some insect?

I see. Definitely not an insect, a mammal for sure. I guess I feel like this whole long walk out here is the daydream.

What about your dreams themselves? When you sleep? Are those any different than the dreams you have in your waking life?

Anna watches Gabe as he hesitates to answer. Perhaps his recent dreams have been different, but he isn't ready to share with her quite yet. She offers relief by answering in his place.

I do remember my dreams more clearly out here, when I wake up. They feel more connected to my life, almost as if this place is somehow in between life and dreams.

During dinner, they snack on each others' meals, even off of each others' plates. By now it is customary for her to finish the scraps on his plate. They hear the sounds of others talking back along the trail. It is still quite light out. They have set up camp early this day. She already has played in the dirt, making a sculpture with twigs, leaves and twine, as she has every night previous while with Gabe. Two boys, talking loudly and punctuated with laughter, come into view.

The aura around them is familiar to both Gabe and her. The two boys from a week earlier, they finally have caught up. She and Gabe had made the habit of camping earlier and earlier each day and lost crucial trail time during the cooler hours of the late afternoon. The two boys call out in unison.

Hello. Hellooo!

It's you two. You guys are camping here?

The boy asks with a tone of familiarity as if they all know each other, simply because they had met briefly once before. She feels a scratch of unease in having a light shone on the fact of her traveling with Gabe. Gabe nods hello and seems to wait for her to speak first to them. She does, and after sidetracking the conversation away from why she and Gabe have camped together and for how long, she decides that she is excited to see them again.

We've already eaten. But if you guys want to camp here too, there is plenty of flat ground around. We already have a fire going.

Sure.

Thanks.

They set up. Gabe helps with their tent while she cleans up the pots. She offers them the extra water she has gathered, since it is getting darker more quickly than they have anticipated. They all sit together as they eat.

What's that over there?

What?

By the tree there? We noticed something like that a couple of days ago just near another campsite. Did one of you make it?

Yes. That would be me.

Cool.

Gabe had not asked about her structures but showed much appreciation while watching as she made them and even more so after they were complete. He had sketched one of them in great detail, the first and only recording of any. Darry, the boy with the shorter hair, is the one who had asked and doesn't say anything else about them after that. He is interested only in the facts surrounding the creation anomaly in the midst of the trail. Rich is the other boy, the one with the longer hair. He just smiles, nodding in approval.

After a couple of minutes of quiet, Rich asks a question and changes the subject to something Gabe had said earlier as he had stoked the fire to warm up more dinner. Rich makes his inquiry first by repeating, almost word for word, the phrases Gabe had offered as he re-ignited the flames under the wood. Gabe turns, surprised that Rich remembers the words so accurately, and corrects a simple alteration that Rich had made.

Make this light ignite a fire within each of us
And spur us to bravely seek this place, ourselves and what we need.

Yes, now I remember. I forgot the word bravely.

He has a different one almost every night.

Did you make that up?

No. I have written some of my own. But... those I usually say when I'm alone. I gotta make sure you guys get the best ones, so I fish them out of the records I keep of others' writing. Glad you liked it, Rich. That is definitely one of my favorites and seems to fit well with everything out here.

Darry seems uneasy with the conversation and redirects it to something more immediate. His urge to maintain inclusivity, keep them all drawn together, clearly is a dominant trait.

Hey, do you guys know that we're only about six miles from one of the gaps?

Yeah. We noticed that on the map.

Have you ever passed over it? You can get there by foot or driving over the mountain. There's a great inn there right off the trail as you cross the street at the top of the gap. We've stayed there before.

Yeah. We saw that too.

We're going to spend the night there tomorrow, Rich reserved a room. It's got room for four people if you guys want to crash there with us.

She feels trepidation about her companionship with these two boys extending beyond the simple courtesy of this evening's arrangement. It feels less serendipitous than it does some form of forced déjà vu, from when both she and Gabe had passed on their first invitation. Even while traveling in the company of Gabe over the past week, she had maintained a sense of isolation. She does not welcome the intrusion, but again she is conflicted. A part of her is still drawn to guys like this, their boisterous nature. Always smiling. Always about to make someone laugh. They are without inhibitions. They are perpetually gregarious. They live on the surface of things and, even in the solitude of the woods, they find a way to make it a party.

Are you sure?

Absolutely. The pub's fabulous, and every weekend has live music.

Tomorrow is Friday.

We planned our whole hike around arriving there tomorrow. Those rains almost hurt us. We were worried, but we booked it the last five days, barely stopping at any of the summit points and setting out right when the trail was visible.

I haven't slept on a bed in weeks.

She tries counting the days in her head.

That's very generous of you.

Gabe's tone is cordial.

I would like to contribute though. Either for the room or for your meals.

Don't worry about it. The room's cheap. It's more of a hostel than an inn. The rooms are sparse, no TV or anything.

Gabe does not try to dodge the invitation either. The question had been decided when she accepted. The two of them felt it. A partnership in their travels had been cemented.

The extent of that partnership is revealed the next day when the four of them carry their backpacks into the small brown room located in a low rectangular building adjacent the main inn and restaurant. The room is listed as accommodating four people. Upon entering, the sleeping arrangements are clear to everyone without discussion. Darry and Rich set their packs by the bunk beds, and Darry tosses himself immediately on the lower bunk. He lets out a sigh of comfort, as if the days he had spent in the woods were not by choice. That leaves a double bed across the room for her and Gabe to share. She goes around to the right side of the bed and sits. She sets down her pack on the floor and begins the ritual of preparing her place. Gabe goes to the other side of the bed but doesn't spend more than a minute before rising and going to the door with his pack left unopened.

I'm going out to explore the inn. He doesn't offer for anyone to join him, but his tone does not seem to exclude the possibility.

I'm gonna shower.

I got it next.

She decides to go with Gabe as the other two clean up.

Wait up. I'm coming to.

Don't feel like you have to join me.

I don't know. I feel strange being in there while they shower and change... alone. She pauses then. I know they are really nice and seem trustworthy. I just...

She pauses again.

Haven't been in a room in awhile?

Yes. I think that's what it is. I haven't been in an enclosed space with anyone for some time. They walk a little further, and then she continues.

What do you make of them? Did you ask anything about them last night? I went to bed early, but I could hear muffled sounds, like the three of you were talking.

Yes. Darry did offer up some details of his life. Rich too. I don't know. They came out for a couple of weeks before their jobs begin. Both of them start work in Boston next week. Something or another in the financial world, and the other is in fundraising. They didn't say much, since they haven't started yet. I guess they've been looking for work since graduating and taken advantage of the time to go on some trips this summer. They're roommates and went to college together.

What about you? What did you tell them?

I said that I wanted to travel some more and, when I finally decide to stop, I'll move somewhere because of its geography, not a job. I don't plan on living in a city.

I know what you mean. I would miss the mountains too much. I need to see lots of green out the windows.

Their conversation reaches its limit concerning the distant future. They pass through the large doors of the old inn. Off to the left is the tavern and a large eating area with mostly small round tables for two, some four person booths and a couple long tables. A band has already set up their instruments in the corner, and lights are shining on the make-shift stage. No one is in there yet except an older couple sitting at the bar. The bartender is out of the room even. Straight ahead is an old ornate staircase that winds up to where other rooms must be. Nicer ones, she decides, for the non-hikers. To their right is a passageway to the innkeeper's desk. A large built-in bookcase of dark wood takes up the entire wall and has an aura reminiscent of her college professor's offices. This one emits something else though, a hint of a mystic's library. She walks over to it. The books are the first things she has encountered since arriving out of the woods that make her glad to see civilization again. The dank, brown room where they were staying had put her off some, as well as the many cars parked up by the inn. But the long wall of books reminds her of humanity at its best. She eyes one that juts out from its peers on the nearest shelf. A Guide to Hiking the Appalachain Trail. Another one right by it, a Guide to the Long Trail. She passes over them and sees a third book, recently perused by someone, A History of Witchcraft in New England. The book is a hardcover with an antique quality to it. Its pages are filled with Pagan symbols. It is not a typical history book. She perceives that, in its essence, it approaches the topic of witchery as something real, some lost forgotten art or folk custom to be rediscovered, like making furniture by hand or growing cold weather vegetables. She puts the book down and returns to the titles on the shelves. More strange books appear. Many about Ireland. About early New England. Old books. Ones unlike those in college libraries or even town libraries. Some books seemed absurd. Stories of strange occurrences. Celtic rituals. Political books divergent from academic rhetoric or mainstream newspapers. The chairs around the room have an antique quality and match the character of all the literature in the room. Gabe sits on an old, firm sofa chair upholstered with red tapestry. He looks at the books on a nearby table. He begins reading from the first one he finds.

This place is interesting.

It is…

Off-trail magic?

Sort of.

Did you see the pictures on the wall.

No.

In the pub. There are newspaper clippings from all sorts of moments in Ireland's history.

Interesting.

She shrugs.

Gabe continues reading. She grabs a book from a shelf, one which she is certain never to find again outside of this place. Circa 1900. No one enters the inn or comes and goes from the room. They read in silence for a half hour or more until Darry and Rich come up to the inn's porch. Laughing. She and Gabe hear them, and drift back from the pages in their hands. The boys come to the edge of the quiet scene and are unsure how to enter it. They halt the momentum of their thoughts, hushing their laughter to just smiles.

If either of you want to shower. It's all yours.

Gabe looks over to her. She doesn't flinch from her book. He waits. She isn't responding, so he rises and makes his way to the door. She finally speaks.

I'm in no hurry to shower. I want to read.

Gabe exits. Darry and Rich rummage through the room, picking up books and reading the titles. Darry finds a cache of games and pulls out a homemade checkers board. Rich joins him in setting it up, and they begin to play. Once the game is underway, they begin talking again. Then laughing. She reads quietly still.

Sometime later, after she has showered and returned to the inn, they all sit down in the restaurant pub area. A round of Guinness is brought to the table. They order food, fish and chips and burgers for the boys. She orders something vegetarian. They order more beers, and then the music begins. The band's signature sound is emanating from a young woman's mandolin. She is clearly the most accomplished player up there. They play folk songs with a bluegrass feel but also a hint of modernity in the harsh strumming of chords and rock-like speed. Then, Irish folk songs. At one point, a woman stands up and starts dancing. Just with her feet, very Irish. She dances again after a time, and she is noticeably more drunk. The four of them tell stories of hiking, polishing the details of the hardships to the point of romance now that comforts are presently at hand, including the luxuries of cooked meals and freshly tapped beers. Darry drinks excessively. Rich moderately. She and Gabe stop after two beers and both get sleepy. At one point the music crests, and the whole bar seems to be swaying and partaking in song, Darry stands up and shouts a sort of Irish yee-haw. Rich laughs uncontrollably. Gabe blushes but smiles nonetheless. She wishes that she too could lose control like Darry. She reasons that the flair for rowdy animation requires a certain personality or a certain quantity of alcohol. It is undeniably attractive right now. Her eyes are set on him. She keeps her smile alive, waiting for the next outburst of spirit to infuse the space around him. With the next song, the evening finds its real pinnacle in the familiar anthem of a particular generation. As the band interprets "Wagon Wheel," the audience delivers its finest performance of the night in each chorus of the song and with the short refrain of "up in New England."

Afterwards, the whole night softens as it dissipates. The music fades from rebel tales to waltzy ballads. Nothing is linear at this hour. Conversation is erratic, and it is unclear how all the events come to pass. Talking one minute to Rich about the contour of one woman's large body and breasts. Next Darry is commenting about the Irish economy and how different the people there are from those in the rest of Europe. Somehow, the more he drinks, the more sober his conversation. The social niceties of drunk pub life is what he knows best, it seems. The way in which he communicates with the waitress and the bartender are evidence of his lifelong experience with bar life. He draws a barrage of others to filter in and out of their group. The most conspicuous of those is a middle aged French-Canadian couple. They speak little English and have a heavy accent. Rich studied French in college and tries talking with them. It is a struggle. Later, he tells the group that they don't speak proper French, he cannot understand them. His comment bothers her but she has drunk too much to take it too seriously. They are nice people, she says. She watches their unfamiliar mannerisms. They are hiking the entire Long Trail, from North to South, in the opposite direction. They discuss Quebec and hold a strong nationalistic pride in their expressions. Gabe listens while staring at the many stories posted on the wall, reading old newspaper clippings from thirty, forty, even fifty years ago.

Finally, they all head back at the same hour to the room. Rich climbs up to his bunk with some difficulty. Darry reels forward to the lower bunk, shedding his clothing along the way, until he is in his underwear only. Gabe gets into his side of the bed without stumbling. She searches her pack for something to sleep in and goes into the bathroom to change. She joins Gabe in their bed and feels his presence beside her. Their bodies do not touch exactly. The weight of the others limbs and the intimacy of being under the same sheets together normally would rouse something like either of trepidation or desire in her. But tonight, because of the long hours and alcohol, she slips comfortably into this scene with him. There is something almost familiar about lying next to him in bed, half naked and almost touching.

I want to do something. It's just… I don't want to decide what to do based on reasoning alone.

You can't do nothing.

Do something great, I mean. I feel that my ideas need to be validated by experience, or they are simply illusions I have conjured.

She had returned to their room the next morning after breakfast in the inn and encountered this conversation.

Something great, like what?

He pauses for a moment.

Change things? I don't know. I suppose change is an illusion itself. I want to make something that wasn't there before. Create… a culture. An idea born of reason, fermented in experience and then distilled to something great.

Gabe turns the question back towards Darry.

Why do you want to go to Boston? What are you seeking there?

A career.

A pause.

Money.

Another pause.

Build a life for myself and, eventually, a family.

Darry smiles.

It is clear to Anna that life for Darry is in some ways a game approached with the motivations of a boy. He wants to see what he can win for himself. But she knows that he is, like so many others she knew in college, someone who has a hardened thread of responsibility running through his core. He wants to possess enough wealth and power to command a certain life to unfold for him. To not venture forth in this way would be an insult to everyone that had sacrificed for his sake. He would be selfish to indulge in something intangible and not yet realized in the world, to forge ahead and invent the world around him.

If I was a real risk-taker, I would try nothing else but painting. I would be an artist. That would be the greatest risk, not the whim of a daydreamer. I too want a life where I can have and give things. I want to make money of course.

Gabe's declaring his desire for financial success also has strands of boyish gaming, but he does not seem to interpret his imagined gains as winnings. They are necessities for the creation of a world and life that would have meaning. That is his aim, she decides.

Rich is not engaged as he finishes packing up his things, but she is sure he has been listening. She wants to ask about it all, know how it was that the conversation began, but she can see that Gabe is tired of talking. Darry's voice has gotten louder and, unlike last night when it needed to rise against the noise of the band and throngs of people, it has no competitors in the room. Maybe some of Gabe's points are lingering there silently, and Darry feels he must speak volumes in order to squash them once and for all. Whatever the reason, his voice is there now, speaking loudly and telling stories.

I've decided not to head north on the AT.

Anna's announcement ends their discussion.

I just was reading in the inn about some places on the Long Trail and think I might head that way.

It has not been discussed if they will travel on together. She has not learned which way Gabe is going. What she does know is that Darry and Rich are meeting someone in New Hampshire in a few days and will get a ride back to Boston.

Gabe turns from his deliberations with Darry, and his eyes widen with a delight she has not before seen in him. Gabe had grown quiet since joining up with Darry and Rich, in a way that was different from his aloofness before on the trail. Now it is clear that a pinch of jealousy had been stirring in him. Only a trace amount, a gradation that had passed the notice of everyone but her. She is sure of it. Whatever stands guard over his heart is starting to waver. He is happy, and she knows that he too must be travelling the Long Trail.

Why are you so focused on reason. I think the heart trumps reason.

She says well after the conversation has dissolved into the muted sounds of packing.

The moment of parting comes as suddenly as their meeting by that campfire in the woods two nights before. Unlike the easy spontaneity of linking their journeys together, separation feels uncomfortable. They all barely know one another. They offer one another email addresses and write out their full names for one another to see for the first time. It is an odd feeling to learn someone's full name only as you say goodbye to them. They snap some group photos, standing together where the trails split in two directions. The three boys together, with her in the middle, holding the camera out to take the shot.

Darry invites them both to visit anytime in Boston. Rich hugs her goodbye. Then he hugs Gabe too. Darry waves. And then the two pairs diverge.

The universe of the woods is doing what it does best, whittling down groups into smaller groups. And now too, the unexpected follows them into the forest, seeking to carve away still more. Within minutes of walking together, once again just the two of them, a young boy only about fifteen years old comes running up the path towards her and Gabe. It is not uncommon on certain parts of these mountains to see an occasional runner traversing up and down for exercise. They step to opposite sides of the trail to let him pass but notice he is wearing jeans. He slows down and stops between them.

Are you Gabe?

He manages the words between deep inhales and exhales.

Yes.

There's a message for you back at the inn.

What is it?

The boy keeps breathing fast, but it is clear he has recovered and is simply avoiding Gabe's inquiry.

Did you take the message?

Yes.

Well?

The boy's face becomes flush, and his demeanor tell them both that the role into which he has been thrust is unfamiliar to him. The adult in him rises up, commanded forth for the first time by the gravity of the news he has been charged to deliver.

Your mother has been trying to reach you. Your grandfather is in the hospital, and they need you to get there immediately. I'm sorry.

The boy breathes normally now and stands straight up as he communicates the message. She has been watching the young boy's face as he speaks. Now, turning to Gabe, she sees the alarm and urgency in his facial nerves.

Is there someone at the inn that can drive me to the nearest bus station?

I can. I'm the only one there right now.

How old are you?

Gabe asks and, for a moment, the look of fright leaves his face only to return swiftly.

Gabe and the boy turn to go back down the trail and off the mountain. The moment does not grant the opportunity for a hug or a proper goodbye. He mumbles something, but it is in their eyes that the parting is made. Nothing about when they might talk again. Just a sadness felt, heard, and shared. She gazes down the trail as he jogs alongside the boy. Once his figure is no longer within sight, she stares a moment longer and imagines that Gabe is now invested in the news of his dying grandfather and the speed he must make to get there. She flashes forward to him getting in the boy's car. Then at a bus stop. Climbing up onto a bus and throwing his backpack up in the overhead compartment. Riding somewhere, to a town, to a car he has parked somewhere. Then his driving fast down a highway. Windows down, air whipping into the car. Stopping only for gas. Racing to that bedside. Where his mother and father, maybe a sister and brother, maybe others, are all gathered waiting for his arrival. Before his grandfather passes. She imagines all of these moments, like blazes of lightning striking one after the other.

Then she cannot see any further into what comes next for him. She sees herself standing there alone on the trail again. She wonders if she should have gone with him, at least down to the inn. Absurd questions float up to the surface of her thoughts, but she doesn't attempt to answer any of them. The feeling of abandonment is peculiar and illusory. She was not left here. The forest had brought them together. She remembers one of the nights when she and Gabe had camped alone. He said something about the eternal. It feels eternal here. She is now on the other side of that statement. How is she supposed to walk away from the abruptness of life? How strange it is suddenly to be alone. Feeling a heightened sense of this instant, she is conscious of everything. Of having happened upon Gabe in the first place. Of the night before in the bar. The books in the inn. The dancing drunk woman. The three boys, all of them. Would she contact any of them? Would they her? Would she keep going? Or not? Either way, she feels a pang of unease. There is no way to describe it.

She sets herself on course, deliberating in her thoughts. Her treads are considered and delicate. Minutes pass. The feeling of walking settles in again, and she finds a passageway out of the oddness of Gabe's departure. She does not make her way fully through it, but enough that she is able to continue her journey. She looks about. Sees the trees once again. The sun falling all over the forest floor like a Jackson Pollack painting. Splotches of bright yellow light amidst the varying hues of green, brown, blue, purple, black, everything thrown out onto the collage of growth all around her. The trees stand tall and unaffected by what's taken place. Their branches sway tenderly, making a mother's hush sound for her baby. The footpath, laid out before her by the help of countless others, dedicated outdoorspeople, appears like a ladder set against the earth's rooftop. If she climbs that steep incline to its final step, she will be perched on life itself. All reflections of her past and premonitions of her future will be visible in that expansive view of the universe. As an exposé, a grand rendering, a telling of significance. Only she does not grab hold of its edges and begin clambering up its chute, stricken with summit fever. Instead, she scales that inclination knowing that any epiphanies met at the top would require that she stay present, allowing memories and hopes to arise and be absorbed by the trail

She encounters a print and stops. The marking of a raccoon or beaver. She looks for more. Dried leaves cover the surface of the ground, just beyond the trailhead. No chance for more tracks with the ground so dry and with an animal so lightweight. She stares along the print's bearing, imagines the animal's route. She sees him scurrying past tree limbs and rocks. Under branches and over piles of leaves. Tunneling through ferns and plants twice his height. He ducks around a large tree, keeping out of sight from other animals. Not wanting to be spotted by another species. Even an encounter with one of his own kind might have unpredictable consequences and prove unfortunate. Best not to risk being vulnerable. Where did he go? She wonders. The forest reveals at one moment and reclaims in the next. All the while she is there, walking this human pathway sown by others like her who hope to discover, experience, pursue a purpose or wander with none at all.

... the whole of nature is a
metaphor of the human mind.

—Emerson, *Nature*

A day passes. Maybe two. She keeps moving from shelter to shelter, from peak to peak, from one side of the mountain to the next.

The trail begins to resemble another part from weeks ago. The oversized boulders on her left. The winding turn up ahead. Tall trees stand back from the footpath with branches appearing not less than fifty feet from the bases of the trunks. They appear like ship masts all raised one next to the other. They are buffered with short brush rising no higher than six inches from the ground. Some kind of plant species that smothers the earth, allowing no sunlight beneath its greenery, leaving no hope for other species to grow in its midst. The whole scene evokes a memory, and she is acutely aware of every detail because of its similarity to some point in the past. She scrutinizes the stacks of boulders, seeking to discover a difference between them and the images recalled from her memory. She follows their lines, weighs their mass in her mind, calculates the grade to the top. She dwells on their subtle shade of purple-gray. She knows they never will be illuminated the same way again in the light of a different day.

The oddity of the moment climaxes as she ascends into the second scene, which matches every corner of her past without distinction. The feeling could be déjà vu but for its remarkable persistence. No one is there to discuss whether it is in her head alone.

It will end up ahead, she tells herself.

She hypothesizes that, after so many hours spent wandering paths in the woods, the probability of finding such commonalities is strong. The variables here seem too immense to allow for it though, unlike with the patterns and symmetries of a metropolis. Her strides begin to stretch time. Her consciousness grows even as her mind records the infinite details of the moment. This awareness bonds her to the present in such a way that the previous days, weeks, months, and even years appear to have been lived by someone else.

She continues farther up the trail. It clears a new direction for her to pursue. The feeling does not subside but evolves further, most peculiarly, as she is now able to discern with complete accuracy what will come next. As if hearing a song for the first time and being able to hum along, hitting every note as it were revealed. Somehow. Both an intuitive sense and a calculating science reveal the next root at her feet and the next turn before her. It all transpires without her sanction, but she does not resist it. The thought does not cross her mind. What takes shape in her cannot be described in words or images. She is aware that being solitary is essential to this awakening. The same way the notes of the tune follow one after the other, each step she takes has a rightness.

The air ascends the mountain with her like a companion travelling the same speed, making the same turns, and aiming for the same destination. When she slows, it slows. Where she stops, it stops. If she could leave the present moment and find her way back to the rains, to the pestering black flies and merciless humidity, she would see how much this moment differs. Nothing fights against her. All her doubts about the reasons for this or that dissolve into the air around her. If before she had been a stranger in this world, now she is as much a part of it as the trees, the rocks, the path itself. Illuminated by the sun, her hues vary slightly like the boulders on the trail. The breeze does not carry her or push against her, but accompanies her. She could not believe in the supernatural before this moment. She would not believe it later that day and certainly not months from now. Not in the same way at least. Bearing witness is temporary. It happens in brief, momentary bursts. Belief may be absurd, but it is awe-inspiring when it takes hold. It allows her to transcend her individual self and see, with mathematical precision, the fate of everything. The all of everything. Each detail of the universe revealed with equanimity. She sees the sun break through the clouds in a majestic fashion. It is just light. It is a simple transpiring moment of nature. Believable. But what it conveys is boundless.

A flock of birds streaks through the opening. Their flight pattern is chaotic at first, until they settle and float just above my head at the rim of the tree tops. They circle. They are crows. Only crows would circle like that. They make no sounds, which makes me wonder what they are doing. I keep moving up the path. I focus my eyes straight ahead. Wait a minute. Look up again to see that the birds are still there, quiet and circling. The spell that has infused the world I inhabit is coming more into focus. In a different circumstance, I would shy away with apprehension at the crows. Their activity would mean something. But nothing to do with me. Are they following me? Or am I following them? I am inclined to follow them. They keep above the footpath until I reach a clearing at the top of the ridge. I stop there and stretch out along a rock face that leans to the west. The sun bathes me in light. Shadows dance upon my skin and the rock's smooth surface. The crows circle above me still, as if waiting for me to make the next move. As if waiting to be told where they should go next. I watch them out of the squint of my eye. Silhouetted by the white light of the sun, they flicker in my vision without making a sound even in the flapping their wings. I know that I cannot command them but feel profoundly connected right now. I watch the events around me unfold and am charmed by my ability simply to notice.

With a swift change in course, the wind sweeps over the rock face in a rush. She lifts her back off the hard surface and opens her eyes wide to watch the crows fly down the mountain in a crooked line, making loud caws. The spell is broken. The feeling lifts. The direction in which the crows fly is all that is left for her to wonder about. She watches them swoop down until they disappear into the open valley below.

There are many individuals who stand out on the trail, but most adhere to the mountain climber or backpacker persona. Their gear serves to conjure a sense of luxury in the sparse living of survival in the wild. In some ways, it is impossible not to succumb to such trappings when taking on the monumental task of walking for weeks through the wilderness. There are those who keep to themselves and make their way with unassuming trail names and no fanfare, rarely mentioning even how far they have come already. Even they must carry at least some of the indicators of the outdoors culture. But there was one. He never crossed paths with her or any of the others she met, but all of them had heard about him. He had been on the trail and finished while she was still somewhere out there. She met a couple one afternoon at a common stopping ground and listened to the story as they ate their lunches together.

We didn't meet him. We had just missed him on the trail leading down from Maine to New Hampshire. I don't know how we didn't see him. We certainly couldn't have missed him. I'm sure he would have stood out.

Wait, you should tell her about the girl.

Yeah, so this girl who met him, we did run into her. She was around twenty or so, in college. She was by herself, not hiking the whole trail or anything, just out for a couple of days. She met up with him, and they camped one night together.

The couple telling the story to Anna speaks as if the characters are unique enough to warrant a long recounting of as many details as they can remember. The boy punctuates the story with brief interruptions to remind his girlfriend of certain points that she might miss or to add some detail that he feels is worth the extra emphasis. There is something about being told a story by two tellers versus one that has always fascinated Anna. She listens closer and is more apt to be transported into the world of the story if both tellers seem equally enthralled by the characters. It paints a vivid picture to see.

The best way to describe her is… she was not only the sort to have every Joni Mitchell album, she was a perfect replica of Suzanne. You know the song, right? Free-spirited, pretty girl. A natural sort of pretty, who can draw things out of anybody with her smile. So she meets him one night as she's getting ready to set up her tent. This young guy walks up with barely anything on his back. As he sits there with her, he snacks on snickers bars and drinks a can of cheap beer. She can't figure out where he got it. He's wearing sneakers without socks and a bathing suit as his hiking shorts. His tent is a complete wreck. He doesn't seem to be at all prepared to camp, literally has no survival things with him at all. Nothing. She thinks he must be a day hiker who decided to try camping a night.

When she told us this story, we noticed that she was not the most prepared hiker either. So if that's any indication, he must have looked really odd for a thru-hiker.

Yeah, that's true. She learned that he always had a can of cheap beer in his hand, even while hiking along the trail. He would crunch up the empty can and stuff it into his pack. It was as if that was the only real purpose for the pack. He had hiked the entire Appalachian trail like this, but what's even more crazy is he was doing it at a ridiculously fast pace. He didn't bring any of this up with her. She discovered it only after really prying into him. She was completely taken aback when he revealed how far he had gone. Everything about him had, up to that point, made her think he was just out for a spontaneous hike, and ill-equipped for even that.

She thought he was just going up Katahdin, which is actually a pretty serious day hike.

She told us the story of this guy, and you could tell she had been telling and retelling it.

What did he look like?

She said he was in good shape, definitely an athlete of some kind. Maybe a rugby player. He wore a rugby shirt at night. He had light brown, almost blonde hair. Not short but not long either. She said it was hard to know if he had curly hair, or if the weeks of not washing had made it super wavy. Beyond that, she just said he was really good-looking, which we could have guessed, the way she told us the story.

She was clearly into this guy.

Do you think he just shed his clothing and gear along the way?

Or maybe, he gave it away to others he met who needed things?

Yeah. We don't know. She didn't say.

She learned the craziest part right at the end of their short time together: that his girlfriend... yeah, he had a girlfriend... she was in a coma.

What?

I know. Crazy, right? She had been in a coma, and the likelihood of her waking up was completely unknown. But they predicted that if she did, she would most likely not have suffered any serious loss of brain function or anything.

So why was he out hiking for so long, while she was in the hospital? That doesn't seem right.

That's what this girl thought too... at first. The thing is, they were supposed to hike it together.

Well, that seems even worse, that he would leave her?

I know. He said that he had stayed with her a lot, but her parents thought he still should hike it. He confessed that he was having serious difficulty handling the whole situation. He was kind of losing his mind with the not knowing and all the anxieties around it. They thought it would be good for him. He said he wanted her to hear his voice every day though and just couldn't imagine disappearing for so long.

So what finally led him to be able to go?

The girl's mom suggested that he speak into his cell phone every day, send the audio to her, and she would play his voice to her in the hospital. He was always rushing towards places where he could charge up and get service. He said, every minute he spent out on the trail, he felt this unbelievable pull to get back into range, to get any news and also to send her his voice diaries.

That is amazing. But, her parents would hear them too? That must have been uncomfortable.

He didn't consider that until the first time he sent a recording. He listened to it a couple of times before sending it to his girlfriend's mom, wondering if it would be appropriate. But the intensity of the whole thing apparently wiped away any worries.

He raced through the mountains, through all those states, with a superstitious hope that she would wake up when he completed the whole thing. He was nervous, though, that she would be upset he did it without her.

How did she end up in the coma? Did this girl ever find out?

Yeah. This girl was the sort who could ask anybody about anything, no matter how personal. She could do it in a way that was so kind and empathetic. I'm telling you, she was like Suzanne. She found out they were in a car accident. His girlfriend had been driving, and a deer ran in front of the car. That is all he said. He wasn't badly hurt. She actually didn't get hurt other than the head injury that led to her coma.

So why the beer? Why the sneakers and bathing suit?

All she could guess was that he wasn't really thinking about much except for her. He clearly wasn't worried about his own situation.

He must have had a lot of trail angels helping him.

I'm sure.

It just seems too unbelievable that someone could hike so far with so little and all the wrong things. It seems like some kind of story that, if you made it up, no one would believe it.

But, you want to believe, for the sake of his girlfriend.

I know. I wonder what happened when he got back to her.

Yeah. I wonder what he said in all of those recordings. It's one of those rare connections formed by extraordinary circumstances. They share something so intense, even if it seems one-sided. I would imagine that type of bond isn't even formed in all marriages.

Crazy. So is that all you know? Did the girl who told you the story know the ending, about his return home or anything else?

No. That's all. We don't even know the last name of the girl we met, and she didn't know the last name of the boy she met. That's all we'll probably ever know about him and his girlfriend.

It's just so odd to carry this guy's story now, to know something so personal and sad about a stranger.

The couple finishes telling me their story. I wonder, as they sit close to one another, grasping a little at one another's arms and sides, what this story means to them. Here they are, hiking the same trail that this crazed boy did, but together and of sound mind, content with the fortunate circumstances they share together. Perhaps the story lets their minds wander to a ledge somewhere, where they have a view of the sublime, where the precariousness of life is within sight. They experience the history of one man and realize they can share in it, live by the story's edge, close enough to feel the fright and hope in it, knowing what the steep drop-off represents but resting safely planted on solid ground. I won't remember much about the couple except for the story they carried with them. I will have whittled down the details so much that only the recordings of a boy remain, ones that I have filled with my own voice and thoughts, sent along to a distant partner, who woke up and finally heard all the things I have discovered about love and connection and the now, what I have discovered of the tender and indomitable bond that comes from the experience of suffering.

A week passes. A cold front slips in over the night, a reminder that things are changing. Soon these mountain tops will be frosting in the dark hours and setting dews in the morning as heavy as rainfall. She would not have made it to Katahdin's sharp edges of rock and tundra even if she had stayed on the Appalachian Trail. They would have to wait. Her moods are calibrated to the lower elevations of the Green Mountains. The valley below is spectacular to behold and comes into sight like a delivery from another world or, more accurately, like a deliverance into that cradle of quilted farmland. The lives below draw her nearer. The valley doesn't feel so distant. She can see herself down there. In the open. Walking through a field. By a barn. Driving down a road between the shades of hayfields waiting for their final cut, before the fullness of autumn blankets the earth. The view of grazed and harrowed land cuts to something basic in her.

Weeks before, she and Gabe had happened upon an orchard where the trees were ripe, and the readiness about the harvest in that spot of dirt struck a similar chord in each of their minds. Standing side by side, each felt the other experiencing it like twin minds converging upon the same plan. And in their twin minds, nothing felt strange about it. They looked at one another, then to the clear view framed out by the gnarly branches bearing the weight of the fruit. The horizon gleamed every color but darkness, and they could see through to every moment that was to come. Somehow. Not to a place. Nor an image. It was a feeling. And it was here again with her. It had not gone away from her like so many thoughts she had left scattered along the trail to be drawn back into the soil. This one had reached that inner most column, the one running through her whole body, commanding her mind and orchestrating her limbs ultimately to the direction she would choose.

It is now that she stands, puts her backpack on, and heads away from the white blazes painted two by six on trees and rocks. She turns in the direction of the blue markings which lead down a side trail, territory not trespassed by thru-hikers or purists. What of it, she doesn't consider herself anything in particular. The path isn't different. Its obstacles and pleasures are the same after all.

The cool air carries lighter reflections. The burdensome heat and torrential rains feel more like a story to her now, something linear and full of metaphor in which she is herself a character. She passes the time trotting in a familiar pattern down the mountain. Her young and capable legs guiding each placement of her feet dexterously. Between loose rocks, altering slopes, roots jutting out from the earth. Over unexpected streams and wet mud, she bounces downward without mistake or hesitation. She observes the trees once more, almost with the eye of one who has already left the forest. A calm nostalgia entwined with a private triumph pierces her emotions. She looks forward and backward through her life. She is not an animal lost in the wood. She is not a visitor any longer. Or even a seeker, quietly building her sculptures alone and unseen. She is becoming less of a character from the past, and more of a familiar being that I know and can almost touch. Not altogether one and the same, but her story resonates in me. However different she is than myself today, she is coming into view. I understand her better.

She passes a shelter. A woman is there. About fifty years old. The woman turns to see who is ambling down from the summit. Her hair is the same as mine, in a way, and, despite the extra weight around her limbs, she has a similar frame and body. She seems to make a similar observation as she smiles to me in a maternal way. She rises up from the shelter and approaches to meet me on the path. We say hello to one another. The residue of an accent draws from her lips as she says her name.

Kate.

You came from another direction? You are alone?

She inquires about my entire time on the trail. Still unable to place her accent, I ask where she is from.

Here. Just down this trail. On the foot of the mountains, just before the valley there. I have a little house.

But your accent?

I moved here five years ago. I am from Norway.

I want to ask her why? I have never met anyone who has left Norway. She laughs. Agrees.

I came here for a man. But he died. I am not ready to go back just yet.

Your English is incredible, you sound like you are from Minnesota.

Really? She laughs again.

Her smile has not left her face since our meeting, and I become aware that mine too is just the same. She asks where I am headed. I am not sure.

I wanted to explore the valley and the towns below. I don't know what came over me, I just wanted to leave the woods and the trail and go down there.

Yes, she says. I understand. It is quite beautiful here. That is how I feel as well. Would you like to visit with me, I will make you a special dinner? You could use a home cooked meal I am guessing?

Yes. I would love that.

We walk together down the trail as it evolves from a mountainous forest into a woodsy meadow. We talk about hiking the trails by her home in Norway. She compares the small hills of the Green Mountains to the large glaciered plateaus of mountain that surrounded her there.

The latitude is above the Arctic Circle. It is very isolated there. No people during the winters. It was just me. The three other homes in my town, I would look after while they went south to Bergen. Here, there are always people around in these hills. Winter is still winter. But there are others here.

I answer her questions about my journey and tell her about the boys I had met. She doesn't ask where I am from or about my past, except for my experiences on the trail.

As we near the final markings of blue, I can see sunlight pouring down on some kind of clearing ahead of us. There is no slope left on the trail. We walk as if strolling down the sidewalk in a town. Regardless of the trees and rocky earth, it feels as if we are already out of the wilderness. These woods are the type that live just behind houses and streets. The smell of human civilization seems to penetrate through this point. As we exit the trail, where a box is set against a tree for hikers to sign in and out, there are no paved roads or homes. There is just a calmness that sifts through the air, an indicator that this is no longer the wild but not yet the tame either. She goes to the box and writes her name, Kate fra Norge. I write my trail name down.

We walk down the road to where she has parked her car. On the drive back to her home, we listen to music. She tells me more about Norway and about how all women like myself, six feet and sturdy, should visit there.

It is a land full of very tall women with strong formidable physiques. You will feel small and dainty walking the streets of Oslo.

I laugh. I always have stood out among women.

The men too are well-made, she says.

Well-built, I say.

Both.

Her home is nestled by itself off the road. A feeling spreads in me that I could be in Vermont or Norway at this moment. A strange parallel has been reached. Her home is crisply constructed and taller than it is wide.

Henry built it. He too was a well-made man.

She always smiles when making references about him. No regrets perhaps. Despite having just met Kate, I detect an all-out love in her and know that she holds life dearly each day. Maybe because of a life event long past, or a good mother and father full of life themselves.

I enter her home. Sniffing about, I pinpoint three distinct smells. One wrapped up in the airs of a foreigner, two a roast or stew in the oven, and three a faint history of a man and his tools and things still lingering about. He died of stroke, she tells me.

In his sleep they say, he died peacefully the doctors assured me.

I'm so sorry.

Thank you, you are sweet to visit with me.

You are kind to invite me and share whatever it is that you have cooked.

I know it is meat of some kind. I have not eaten meat in many years and know that I will tonight. I might as well be in a foreign

country. She tells me it is moose stew, the very last of the moose
Henry had gotten last fall. I would have to eat it, and I would have
to enjoy it.

We pass hours together in her home. The sun goes down fast,
and a harvest moon replaces it. A cool, white glow emanates from
the forest outside her windows. Fresh root vegetables from her garden
surround the moose meat and form a sauce that is like nothing I ever
have eaten. Everything has come from her garden and by way of her
husband's good shot. Only a few win the lottery for a license to hunt
a moose, she tells me.

It was his first opportunity, and he succeeded.

She shows me a picture of Henry. He is a solid looking man, tall
but not as stocky as I would have guessed. He looks more like a runner than a hunter.

Where did you meet, I ask her.

Henry was visiting Norway and I spotted him. He had come
in the winter to cross-country ski and see where the Olympics had
been back in ninety-four. In Lillehammer. I was skiing there too. He
stayed for many weeks with me there. Then I visited him here. And I
stayed.

The air is colder than during the last nights I spent camping on
the trail. The loud sounds of insect life have been muted by the coming of autumn. The silence placates my thoughts, and, for the first
time since my wooded voyage began, I feel at rest. The soft cushion
of the sofa massages the muscles in my legs, arms, and back. She
offers the shower to me and the guest room if I would like to stay the
night. I accept. Before going to bed, I sit one last time with her on
the sofa sipping at hot lemon water with honey. She says it is what
she drinks every evening to warm her during cold nights. This time,
she tells me a different kind of story. The smiles and laughs which

have governed her all afternoon and through dinner hush inside of her as she tells me of a young woman that had visited near her home in Norway.

She had been afflicted by something.

Kate stops, makes sure she has locked eyes with me, then continues.

The inner rage of a man.

Again, she pauses.

Something had transpired that she never fully told me about. She stayed only three days in one of the other three houses there in my remote town by the mountains. I talked with her much. But she became less communicative. Then on the third day, that evening she wandered up into the mountains.

Kate pointed up forgetting that outside of these windows was a different range than the one in her story.

She fell asleep up there in the cold. I didn't find her until two days later.

Was she alive?

She went there to die, she tells me with certainty.

Why? How old was she? Did you ever find out what had happened to her?

No. Nothing. I called the police. And I never found out a thing about her.

She tells me this story with a gravity in her eyes, and I bury her words into myself. The woman's spirit lives in this story, I can feel it.

Having it passed on to me, I absorb a part of it into my own sense of being a woman.

Why Kate felt compelled to repeat this story is unclear. Sometimes it is easiest to tell stories to a stranger, to a traveler, and confide in them the things we harbor, the secret tales of our life, the hardest scenes we've witnessed. With those also comes the flood of what we've loved the most and what has loved us in return.

After, I go into the room Kate has prepared for me. The lightness and feminine colors of the sheets and quilt stand in stark contrast to the last interior room I had slept in with Gabe, Darry and Rich. I cover myself with the warmth of everything like a small child searching for comfort and safety in the familiarity of her belongings within the darkness. I hear Kate move about in the other room, settling into the night. The footsteps and sounds of drawers being open and shut resound for me as echoes of the past. The reverberations of domestic life have been absent from me. The clatter of trees, crackling leaves and whispering animals are now replaced with the soft movements of human activity. I do feel like a child again. Is that my mother in the other room? Alone? Am I still ten years old? My dreams are beginning to take shape and mix with the scene.

On the Farm

She stands outside the farmhouse, waiting. The winter air is cold, but the sun is full. Everything is still. A glaze of snow covers the fields and pastures. It has a dim purplish color, almost brown, except where the goat tracks leave bright blue shadows. The expanse stretching from the porch to the distant tree line is interrupted only by the fence. The deep blue streaking beneath it is the most colorful shadow nature can produce. A cool blue-white mountain rises at the horizon. Each element of the landscape she sees only as color, an abstraction.

Only on days like this, with clear rays of sunlight and no wind, will the goats venture forth from the barn. They seem to be without purpose other than to absorb the vitamins from the sun. They roam the alien landscape, wondering what has become of the earth, their grasses. They tell their kids that once it was a green here. There will be green again, and you will eat it soon. Some lick at the snow like dogs, like human children. They squint their eyes at the brightness of the snow crystals, shining like diamond dust and coating all of the earth. All of Vermont, at least.

As she waits on the porch, so too does the whole farm wait for the goats to freshen. This year's kids are not yet born. They have not awaited the promise of green, felt the sun, or breathed the cold air. Nothing begins without the next generation. The bulging doe mothers lie on the hay bedding in the barn, chewing their cud in slow rhythms, staring forward without seeing. The large masses growing off their sides making it difficult to walk, compete in the hierarchy, or butt heads. Some lay unaware of what it is they are awaiting. For them, what is happening to their bodies is as foreign and unexpected as the whiteness outside. But they do not fret about the change. They chew their cud evenly and judiciously, with an eye to the future.

The waiting is a calm. The cold brings a halt to the work that all the other seasons demand. She arrived in this calm, to this farm. This long stretch lasts through all of January and February. It is like the requisite hiatus between long distance runs. It brings rest to the farmers' muscles and joints and recuperation for their minds. She has been told this. She listens each day as they walk past the stacks of hay in the loft, feeding out bales from the first cut. They pull the leaves apart and lean them against the feeders that extend fifty feet long on each side of the barn, the one chore that is constant for every season. Soon, they tell her, the work will begin in earnest. The kids will be bottle fed when they are newly born. The does will be milked once enough of them have freshened to justify turning on the machines. Cheesemaking will begin, and the frantic pace of the farmstead cheesemaker's life will take hold of them all. They will be beholden to the constant flow of milk. To the unrelenting twelve hour cycle of chores. They tell her this again and again. It is hard to feel relaxed in this calm, knowing what could begin any day now.

She recalls their words.

Something happens to us when the animals are dry. There's just the feeding and cleaning up after them. There are still a thousand little things that need to be done, but our routine is on hold. It's difficult to explain to those who have never dairied.

I've come to realize that I feel more awake when I'm busy, even though I might be sleep-deprived. We sleep only an extra hour or so each night, but this whole time feels a bit of a slumber. The activity of life is replaced by reflections on life as a whole.

They discuss more. The conversation jumps to other realms, back and forth from this world to others. Turns to ideas left unfinished from past conversations. New thoughts arise. Answers to questions are revealed. This is how they speak, especially him. His world is mixed, fragmented by the nonlinear thoughts of an unmitigated philosopher. He speaks in contradictions, with uncertainty and deliberation. His words wander like a hiker without a trail.

He confesses.

The idea of doing something great... at some point, it was set in me, like a stone embedded within another mass of rock. It cannot be extracted without compromising the whole of me. But what am I really saying? At that early age, when I was told that I would do great things, did I ever have a clear definition of this great something? Was it laid out before me in subtle ways? Was my mind receptive enough to comprehend what it meant? This idea does not reside in the rational mind. It is pure emotion.

His wife interjects.

When we are milking, we work. Each night, no matter what our thoughts, we fall asleep in an instant. Free from our worries, our doubts, our fears. Our egos are not fires that burn at all hours and need to be filled like the furnace does with wood. We are set on the ground by this task. We must do it. We must do it at an exact hour of the morning and at the same hour of the evening. If we are ill, we still must milk. If we receive an invitation to something, we still must milk. When the world gathered to watch their television screens on September Eleventh, dairy farmers everywhere continued to milk their cows, their goats, and their sheep.

The farmer adds.

The animals are a reminder, at best, of life's continuous demand for our time and labor. They remind us that life is a struggle, no matter what. There is goodness in that struggle. A goodness that keeps us on the ground, living.

Why didn't they place within us a pebble that read good and not great? If you follow our teaching, someday you will do something good. What a relief that would have been. How differently I would have seen it all, as I made my way to this point.

He pauses.

And yet, I wrestle even now with that old stone in me. I explain it to those around me here in this rural, northern state. Only some carry one as heavy as mine. I try to avoid those people as best I can, but only because they are like me. The part of me I am trying to change.

A woman, who had been an Episcopalian minister her whole life, once said to me that she too felt a calling do something great. And yet, she was retired and attending a different denomination from where she had preached. She found herself in the back of a church that was new to her, more focused on humanism than deism. More concentrated on social causes than individual causes. She was a student, a listener. No longer leading a congregation, but a part of one. I told her—the words came out of me and I did not know my own thoughts until I heard them—there is a danger in telling young people that they can do anything. You see, there is an underlying message that goes with that, that they should do everything. Accomplish all of their goals. Fulfill all of their dreams. Satisfy all of their desires.

When the girls are dry, there is more free time for my husband and me. It coincides with the days shortening, and our bodies feel an instinct to rest more. During this time, we feel more in common with the non-farmers—our friends, our extended families, the people in town and the lives we imagine for them.

He sputters one of his large statements with the usual serious look of uncertainty.

The struggle for greatness is perhaps the ultimate philosophical dilemma.

A neighbor down the road there a few miles, she also started making cheese a couple of years ago. She is in the process of deciding on another cheese to make. We discussed the possibilities and, towards the end of our talk, she became less business-like, less scientific, and said I just want to make something that's great. She said it so plainly and with a tone that was so genuine. I realized we aren't farmers, business people, cheesemakers or artists even. We are being human. Living out that condition.

One winter, I think it was 2007, we were waiting. It was February 15, and our breeding schedule had not worked out as planned. Our dry period extended another month than usual. The year before, we had freshened most of our girls by mid-February. The cheese in the aging room was getting as scarce as the checks hitting our bank account. Our state of anticipation transformed to restlessness. We craved waking up early, working harder, milking day and night, being enslaved to the flow of milk.

A Valentine's Day storm had blanketed the whole of Vermont with a deep snow the night before. We started early with our interns and worked all day to emerge from the drifts. We uncovered large swaths for the movement of farm machinery. We had deliveries of milk and grain coming. We carved out paths to the cheese house, to the barns and sheds, and even for the goats to walk outside. We shoveled snow off the roof of our cheese rooms. We dug out the stacks of split wood. The work reminded us of the work to come.

Who is to say what is great? Perhaps it's not to do something great but to reveal the greatness in something.

Life is not a fixed state. On the farm, it follows the ebb and flow of the goats' lives. They are animals after all. Just as we are. They have their first labors, their mothering, their dying. Their times to run out into the pasture to greet spring, jumping into the air, kicking their legs, and throwing their heads back like children at recess. They work out their hierarchy in the herd. Bash each other into oblivion. Then sleep in pairs at night, resting their heads on the backs of their enemies.

It is the biggest mistake an outsider can make, to romanticize farming. Especially dairying. And it is at the same time so absolutely right on. The thousands of us, waking up to bitter cold mornings in the blackness of winter. We do it not for money or lack of schooling. Certainly not for lack of drive. We do it because it is altogether real, and there is nothing you can fall in love with more than what is real. Farming is absolutely full of romance.

The lyrics of his musings ring in my ears. Her practical words pertaining to the facts of the farm also circulate my mind and are stored in the files of my memory.

As the day draws down, and the waiting becomes a chore, a car pulls in the driveway. She arrives. The wait for this one thing is over. The other intern steps out of her vehicle and plants her feet on this spot of earth. Within an hour of her arrival, our first kids are born. Twins. The boy is not named. But the girl they name Claire, named after the young woman getting out of her vehicle right now. The newborn is auburn brown, a rare distinction for a goat and particularly curious considering her mother's coloring and the sire's jet black coat. Claire the young woman, on the other hand, has tresses that match her decidedly.

Claire is unpacking her car when the excitement begins. She drops her bags and heads down to the barn, where the others are gathered around the makeshift pen. The mother, a yearling doe, consumes warm water from a small white pail like her life depends on it. The two kids stand crooked and shiver beneath her big belly. The male, white and black like his mother, has his back two legs sprawled out, successfully balancing on his first attempt. Claire, the female, has more strength in her hind legs, and her posture already resembles that of a properly developed kid. She steps forward. No mistakes. Somehow it all just happens. They are her very first steps. She trusts the ground beneath her, and knows where to walk. With purpose, she moves closer to her mother's belly. Is it smell that drives her? What is it? How does she know to look for food? She nudges at her mother's side, pushing with force against it. It is a demand she makes for nourishment. She pushes again, moving her head ever closer to her mother's teats. The warmth also must play a role in her finding the way to that channel of delivery on which all of her immunities and health depends. Every instinct must be granted and gauged for that finding. Every compass in her workings points to where her sustenance dwells. She punches at the udder with her wet nose and mouth, stimulating the flow of milk to come. She opens her mouth and gums down on the only things her mouth can find, tugs and pulls until finally she draws the liquid into her body. The discovery is absolute pleasure. Her body knows what's right for it based on this feeling of pleasure and satisfaction. Her brother looks at her with his head bobbing in the air. His muscles are at full press in turning to see what she's realized. He is only one foot away from her, and, with one great burst of effort, he lunges himself at the udder that his sister has so adeptly grasped. He falls to his knees and sets his bearings again. Claire has not left hold and continues to drink. Her belly grows visibly as they all watch. The boy stands again and watches more. Then grabs hold of the other teat and finds that sweet ecstasy of need and want being quenched at the same moment. They both will live.

A t night, when the cold is unremitting, my thoughts travel outside our room to the many parts of the farm. The parts that
are covered with this cold. I see the huddled masses of goats, clouds
of warm vapor rising off their backs and from their slow breathing
in the frigid air. Every window is sealed, and the doors are shut. It
is still. Their bedding is soft and dry. I can hear their snores. My
thoughts hover over them.

I see the chickens high up in their coop under the faint glow of
a single fluorescent bulb. They burrow their heads down into their
feathers and don't move at all. They are perched one beside the other,
as if prizes lined up along a mantelpiece, lifeless and stuffed. The heat
from their bodies doesn't steam like the goats.

In an old shed built off the main dairy barn, the pigs are nestled
together in a dark space. There are no windows, and their exit door
is blocked with two square bales. No wind can push inside. The sow's
seven piglets are older now, but still they don't have her ability to
keep warm. They dig under her large belly for a place close to her
warm circulating blood, as if she were a large fireplace with a steady
flame to provide heat for everyone. The steam rising off them is hidden by the dark, but, as my thoughts hover above them, I feel the
faint hint of their warmth passing over me.

As I continue outside over the land, I travel with the northern
wind as it tears past every object, building, and tree. The ground
below is frozen, the heaviest footfalls wouldn't break through the
solid snow mass. I move with the wind, for even in my mind, it is
unbearable to stop and let it scratch over the skin on my cheeks. I
make my way to the old barn by the flooded fields. There are no
trees or bushes. The moon reflects off the fifty acres frozen over with

ice, making everything here visible to my thoughts. The old barn slants and leans in so many directions that it seems to have overcome all efforts to bring her down. It is quiet and strangely peaceful in there. With moonlight coming through the large cracks in the siding. At the same time, it is the loneliest place in the world. I feel miles from home. I feel miles from the dairy barn, where one hundred animals breathe in unison in an effort to stay alive until the horizon turns yellow and orange and the morning sun brings some warmth.

These thoughts will return to me in the morning light and stay with me as I walk and make sounds over the earth's surface. On the frozen land outside. On the goat's bedding. I will lift hay over the fence and pour out grain. Watch as Cat thaws frozen pipes and sends warm water to the animals. He will fix what's broken. Make new what cannot be fixed. Necessity guides him at all times. Purpose does not leave him alone.

The commute that begins their work day is a short walk from the side door of the house, down the driveway and towards the barn and cheese rooms. Approximately fifty long strides comprise this crossing back and forth from work to home, but the passage from one place to the next is not so definitive.

During the summer months, I am told, we will set out before light. If the sky is clear enough, the stars will be visible even as a slight glow hikes over the mountains in the distance and creeps over the fields and trees and earth. They rarely look down as they make their way each day, keeping their heads tilted to the eastern light.

They start down the gray gravel driveway and pass over the path, four foot wide, that the skid steer makes when Cat cleans the barn of its bedding. Spilt manure, compressed by the tires into the driveway, trace the bucket loader's bumpy journey to the small spreader hitched to the big blue tractor. They try their best to avoid the very muddy patches among the dry gravel. Just before reaching the slight incline of a large stone path that leads to the cheese cave's door, they scurry by the chicken coop. Since it is dark, the hens are still perched high up and huddled together. A couple of them let out crows at being disturbed. The path forks at the last eight steps of the commute. To the right is the milk house door. I veer left and over massive slabs of rocks, quarried from the ledge that runs down the middle of the farm, to the door of the cave.

Exposed where the goats play, the ledge marks the beginning of the pasture. On late summer days, when the sun approaches the western sky and its angle is the most dramatic, a warm light paints this rocky formation that grows out of the green earth. At this time, no grays can be found in these rocks, even with the closest inspection. Only vibrant hues of yellow where the sun strikes. Deep purples and blues substantiate the shadowy parts. The ledge runs like the spinal column of this land. A blue ribbon of rock, tying together these structures, these people, and their activity on this solid ground.

I like to imagine what cheeses tasted like three or four centuries ago in Parma, in Northern England, in the mountain villages beside the Alps. The process of making them might have had some similarities to today, but the materials certainly were different. No stainless steel, plastic, or chemical sanitation processes. No pharmaceutical-like laboratories deriving specific and consistent bacteria in powder form. Without refrigeration, cheese would have been subject to nature's temperature shifts, whether in their aging caves or make rooms. I imagine some solidly built cave with old stone and mortar by some mountain landscape. Engineered with thought to the forces of nature: where water would flow when it rained or snow melted, when the sun would shine on the entrance. Harboring within it an ancient ecosystem. Secret strains of mold, white, blue, or orange that would navigate these cheeses to some sacred, eternal flavor that we crave, for which we harbor some primal yearning.

I carry a naked wheel of cheese out from the earth's crust although its smeared rind acts as a kind of clothing. I sit outside with it, exposed it to the natural elements, ready to discover its innards.

The farmer delves.

The fully realized cheese exemplifies man's desire for civilization. But it is an intuitive science born of an idea of civilization that he craves and devours. The flavor is subversively rich, and the textured protein nourishes his appetite for both sustenance and for art, for thought, for life. The flavor on this hill's end by the cave's door is unique and will never be found again. Only I will know it, yet it is impossible to know. Like the histories of common people, it exists only for a brief moment. Its only permanency is in the effect, if any, it might have on the world around it. The cheese teaches me that it is not necessary for your name to be remembered, but instead to have your meaning last.

Traditions usually are passed down from one generation to the next. Sometimes they are discovered in a book by someone altogether different than the one who wrote them down. That person, a foreigner, may take on the task of interpreting it the best she can. At first, she reads it word for word. Mimics the methods. Soon, she makes it her own. She makes her own decisions. We can inherit someone else's culture by our own choice, or sometimes simply by chance. I meet her. I move there. I see that. I decide this. I become that.

Before becoming a farmer, I used to visit others. I would travel far away. To Europe. To South America. To other parts of this country. I was a visitor of culture. I would show up in the middle of the night, unannounced, unexpected, and without anything but a desire to devour everything that charmed my appetite. I would marvel at the differences. I would stare as I walked. At buildings and their intricate sculptures. I visited outdoor markets. I biked into the countryside on the outskirts of cities and walked in farmers' fields. It seemed I could go through life like this, as a visitor of life and be content. But later, after, I wanted to create culture. To merge into life. Root myself into something. Allow a beautiful grove to spring up around me. I would shed the cloak of a visitor and become a steward of culture. And then the creator.

At a certain point, the culture I created took on a life of its own. I had to learn to respect that. Do what it wants, not what I want. Have the courage to get rid of what I love the most, if it doesn't work. When you are creating something new, you must at times risk destroying it if you want it to be great. Then, truly, you will be a creator. He says this firmly and with passion.

One morning soon, Anna will awake to find the definitions of her identity displaced by experiences in the chosen paths of life and, more importantly, those being chosen for her outside of her control. But for now, the narrative of her journey is defined by her alone. Among the dirty mudrooms, the leaning sheds, the bumpy earth of pastures, the unfinished projects of old farmhouses and the odor of hard work is where she feels at home. She delights in the full smiles of people like Elsie. Life's drawing together of these like-minded individuals is what fascinates her most. How was it she found her way to this farm? Why Claire? All of them there, living as a temporary family of their mutual choosing.

Like the story of Cat's name, there is a reason for the coming about of things. Claire asked. It is within her nature to inquire into the stories people carry. With Cat, she is drawn to probe more. He had grown up in a suburban area. Not far from the city outskirts, and not far from the country. He called it the borderland. The mountains spread broadly in the distance, but they were devoid of wildlife. One evening, just before sunset, he was riding his bike down his street. Between two particular houses on this stretch of road lay a hundred yards of woodland on either side with no houses or groomed lawns. This was his favorite place to ride. He would ride its length and back, again and again, like a lion pacing the bars in his cage, pretending it stretched for miles around. The truth is, it was the only woods he knew. But for Cat, at nine years old, it was the door to another world.

Claire washes her hands thoroughly with large globs of anti-bacterial soap. She scrubs and rinses over and over, counting in her head to thirty with each round. She listens both to Cat telling his story and to the water that splashes down from her elbows and falls from her fingers to the stainless steel sink below. The water runs straight from the bottom of the sink onto the epoxy red floor and gravitates to a drain in the floor. All conversations in the cheese room are set against the backdrop of water running, whey dripping, curds stirring, milk agitating. Words are born amidst these sounds of cheese work. Anna repetitiously flips the four ounce cheeses one after another. She slides each one out of its mould and into her palm. She flips it, delicately glides it back into the mould, and places it onto the stainless steel table, where it will sit in the seventy degree air, thick with humidity, for another twenty four hours. Her eyes never leave her task. Just as Claire's eyes methodically gauge the cleanliness of her hands as she washes them. They listen. And imagine young Cat riding back and forth trying his best to escape to somewhere.

The other children in the neighborhood enjoyed the amusements of their backyards, with their pools and finely cut lawns. His sanctuary was that tangle of vine and brush, that world of fallen trees, hidden creeks, and boulders. That small conservation of woods stretched just farther than his young imagination. He could escape. The world, he believed, was accessible from here. Maybe, if he walked from the edge of the road, a clearing would reveal itself after a few miles. A new landscape, with new roads carved along the hills. When he was old enough, in his daydreams, he could go there. And then keep going.

This one evening, by these woods, he earned his nickname. The light was fading fast. As he paced the corridor of tall trees, riding like a boat tacking with the wind, he saw an animal emerge from the side of the woods. It walked from the shadows cast by the sinking sun onto the road. It moved like the cat in his house. It moved with stealth and curiosity. Only this cat was large, a few feet off the ground at the shoulder. They looked at one another for what felt like minutes. Afraid and not afraid. The boy and the cat studied each other, almost greeting one another, before the large animal crossed to the woods on the other side. It moved slowly as it slipped away, disappearing into the maze of tree trunks. The boy pedaled cautiously forward and caught one last glimpse of it. Later, his father said it must have been a fox. But it was some sort of large cat. The young boy retold this story on so many occasions that he earned the name Cat by adolescence.

The cheese room brings forth histories, and these tales of youth at times seem more like reflective confessions than anecdotal tidbits. Ideas ferment alongside the inoculated milk and grow in the mind like blue veins of mold through wheels of ripening cheese. All they need is oxygen to manifest. Like the anaerobic enzymes multiplying with force and flavor, so too are thoughts cultured by the quiet moments of repetitive work. Industriousness of this sort fires the mind and its creative potential. My best thoughts come to me when I'm pouring curds, Cat tells us. Elsie says it's during milking for her. But for Anna and Claire, their minds are fixed on learning the tasks at hand and on ensuring they don't make mistakes.

The rooms have a peculiar quality to them with their smooth white walls and polished cement floors. Temperatures and humidity levels are the defining characteristic for each space. Whereas the make rooms hover between seventy and seventy-two degrees Fahrenheit, the aging rooms have a peculiar qualilty to them, with temperatures and humidity levels the defining characteristics for each space. The rooms are located under five feet of earth and constructed entirely from poured cement, like modern catacombs. Here the cementitious walls are painted white and brightly lit. The first room is the coldest, a large refrigerator to house the fresh and naked cheeses and to dry others before they are moved to their proper environments. The only older cheeses that can survive in such a climate are wrapped or waxed, protecting their moisture levels from the low humidity of this room. The second room is warmer, around fifty-two degrees with a humidity level of eighty-seven percent. This is where young cheeses ripen, the ones that possess enough moisture not to dry out. Their exteriors will grow white mold patiently over a two week span, and they will fully mature in three to four weeks time. The delicate balance of moisture content, temperature and humidity, and the tender care of turning the wheels day after day are crucial to these small medallions becoming fully developed. The third and final aging room is the most primal, the most authentic to the earth and to humanity's distant past. The natural environment at just a few feet below the surface is a cool and humid haven where animals hide from the summer's heat and winter's cold. These are the atmospheres humans have sought for keeping their meats and vegetables from spoiling and for giving their cheeses a world to expand their flavors over months and even years. This last room is also sealed with white walls of smooth cement, but the ninety-eight percent humidity and varying temperatures from fifty-three to fifty-six degrees are products of the earth itself and not manipulated by technology. This place is as quiet as any space could ever be. Dark. Because light too is as damaging to the life in these wheels as are high temperatures or low humidity. Here, an array of molds—white, blue, orange—all grow together and are smeared into one, forming a protective rind on the wheels. Salinity from a brine bath deepens the flavor and cultivates the texture. Here is where the fermented arts still thrive, underground in the dark, cool dampness of the earth.

When Anna works in this last aging room, picking up the eight pound wheels one at a time, turning them, and rubbing them down with extreme care and concern, she loses herself in the task. More deeply than when pouring curds or milking goats. Here, she is unfamiliar with sound. Life scurries about on the earth's crust above her. She doesn't know if the sun is shining, if it's raining. She moves about in this room, performing her task like a monk who has forgotten she has a voice.

Cat barges in, flinging the door open and calling her name, startling her from the unexpected trance of cheese-work. It feels as if he is trespassing into a part of her mind, because her thoughts seem to have drifted out of her and filled the room. She jumps in surprise and almost drops the wheel, which would ensure its demise. Only her acute awareness of its hundred dollar value lifts the spell entirely. He tells her something about what else needs to be done and shuts the door. She returns to her chore but this time does not drift away as before.

On one occasion, Elsie and Cat are going over changes in the work schedule, due to the seasonal nature of things. Elsie has organized everyone's time around the demands of the farm. Cat as usual runs his hands through his hair, fretting over the speed at which everything should be done. It is an unfortunate thing to watch. His frustration seems to lie within his own failure to transfer the know-how required to complete the cheese room procedures efficiently as he himself can. The young twenty-something Cat, Elsie shares, would run from one place to the next, never walking. He moved at the pace of a hummingbird, and the blur of his wings made it difficult for others to observe his methods. It has been quite a transition, having others here to help us along, she confides. It is necessary, but he can't reconcile the varying speeds at which different people move. Some are fast and cat-like, agile, watchful, while others are grazers, ruminating on one thing or another.

It becomes clear to Anna that keeping up with these expectations of timeliness are part of the lesson that she is here to learn. Farmers and cheesemakers engineer efficient processes in order to prosper. A woodworker friend of Cat's once said, anyone can make these tables, these chairs, these dove-tailed cabinets. It might take a hobbyist a year to make a table though. What distinguishes him as a woodworker is that he can make it in eighteen hours. It's true with anything, Cat tells us. What's at stake here is not how to make cheese, but how to create a system that will make cheese.

For Anna, it is ambiguous how all this information fits into her life. She turns it over in her head, trying to understand it all as she prepares meals in the little apartment that she and Claire share on the farm. She weighs it against all parts of her life. Her life presently working on the farm. The interests she keeps to herself. The things she has learned in books. The observations she makes daily in her notebooks. Even her communications with others, her friends in cities scattered throughout the country. Some things stipulate a certain amount of waiting however. They have a slowness about them. Whether it is allowing time for the bacteria to consume the lactose in the milk or for the rennet to coagulate all the milk solids together, some aspects of life cannot be sped up.

Claire reassures her that there will be plenty of time in life to figure things out. To find the answers to the big decisions that each will have to make over the years. Claire's approach in general soothes Anna's appetite for discovering the answers. Anna becomes less of a seeker when around Claire. She marvels at her ability to talk about any subject, no matter how dire or intense, and do it with smiles thrown into mix. She is a warm soul for Anna. Full and uninhibited in revealing her insecurities. She is almost eccentric, if one can be at the age of twenty-three. She walks barefoot to the mailbox over the frozen dirt driveway and wears homemade wool socks at night in the warmth of their shared living space. Nothing bothers her. Nothing about Anna seems to bother her at least. And as a result, Anna reciprocates.

Anna's purpose for being there—learning about animal husbandry, dairying, cheesemaking, running a small business, all of it—is unresolved. Her inclination to venture on this path emerged from the same recesses of her mind that had her hiking indefinitely in the woods. A year ago, she could had not foreseen this coming to pass, but she wonders that perhaps it had been growing in her unknowingly. The thought had been planted there, like it had for so many in her generation who were trying desperately to find an alternative. Some other course. A path that was not as certain. One that would have to be carved out of the tangled woods like on Cat's boyhood street. But was there really a clearing somewhere past the trees? Would there be roads on the other side that one could travel? To find towns populated by people like herself with whom she could commune, live, and love? How many interns like herself at farms like this one, the countless number of farmy institutions out there, how many of us, she thought to herself, would find what it is we are looking for?

Spring comes, but the air does not warm until the season is half over. All of the hundred or so kids born that winter are weaned. They follow Anna around nevertheless, like toddlers running after their mothers, bleating furiously that there is no longer any milk for them. The difficulty of transitioning from child to adolescent comes quickly for a goat. The chores in the barns have gotten easier now that all the maternity pens are empty and the kids don't need bottle-feeding any longer. The pasture is just about ready for them. They meander around the grasses, peering down at the baby blades of grass, and seem to think to themselves, can't I just have nibble already? The earth is their next mother, bearing forth a plentitude of life that will nourish all of them.

Next year, I swear, I am not raising all of these kids. I have to find somewhere for at least two-thirds of them to go. It's just not worth my time.

In the cheese rooms, the rapids of work stream through each cave, in and out of each cheese vat, on and off of each stainless steel shelf. From four ounce columns of pillowy freshness to ten pound rounded blocks of firmed up curd, thousands of cheeses pass through monthly and make their way to the homes of men, women, and children all over New England, New York City and beyond. The caves also are being stockpiled with the reserves of cheese that will be sold through-out the year, especially next winter when the girls are dry again. The months of April and May are the peaks for milk production and, in turn, cheese production. The dance within the cheese rooms is care-fully orchestrated by Cat, and he hurries about like he is still twenty-five years old. Elsie has gotten her wish. The late winter months pain her, haggling with distributors because they are so low on cheese and complaining to Cat that she has to short so many orders. She seems less interested in the money they could be earning and more concerned with satisfying her buyers, the stores, and the restaurants that carry their name on the menu. She wants to fulfill people's wishes, and so wishes for more cheese year after year. By May, the rooms are full enough to grant anyone's order in its entirety. She takes pleasure in filling out the order sheets from this month onward, adding up the sums and totaling all the invoices at the end of the day to see if any records have been broken from the previous year. Although Cat manages the cheese side of things, Elsie firmly holds her finger on the big picture of the farm's operations, commanding her husband on what needs to be made.

Once, after weeks of training and with the manual in her hands, Claire has mistaken a tablespoon for a teaspoon. She adds the appropriate number of spoonfuls of rennet to some cold water and then adds it to the milk when it is ready. The overdose of rennet is discovered the next morning, when Anna lifts the vat's lid for inspection. Only a yellowed, clear whey is visible. She reaches in with her stainless steel pitcher, scoops down into the liquid, and attempts to find the curds which usually are apparent just beyond the quarter inch of whey resting on top of the opaque white yogurty mass. Nothing. What happened? She dunks the pitcher a full foot down into the whey. Still not one curd. She puts the pitcher down and walks fast down into the cave where Cat is writing something in one of the record keeping books. There's something wrong. I don't know what happened, but there are no curds in that batch up there. Oh no, not again. What did that mean, she asks herself? Cat runs up the hallway and back above ground to where the make rooms are. He takes the pitcher without even washing his hands. This signals to Anna that the batch is definitely ruined. He reaches all the way to the bottom of the vat and pulls up a solid mass of strange, hardened curd that look like nothing she's seen before. Even without years of experience, she knows curds should never look that way.

When Cat figures out what must have happened, he holds his hand against his mouth and looks serious. He is not mad. He is calculating everything that must be done. This batch is lost. If he replaces it with tomorrow's batch and moves that batch to Thursday, and then make that cheese Saturday, it will be like this never happened. Only a bookkeeper months from now, in fact eight months from now, would be able to see that any money was lost, and that bookkeeper would have to be analyzing milk production next to cheese production to notice that something was amiss. The good news, Cat tells Anna, is that I'm the bookkeeper. By the time this loss is realized, it will be in the past. So there is nothing to fret about. Then, in a serious tone, so long as it doesn't happen again.

For the next hour and a half, Cat and Anna clean up after the mess, carrying the curds out to the pigs and scrubbing the vat and cheese room floor. Elsie is gone for the day but comes back to do chores in the barn with Claire that evening. When she enters the little shed where the pigs are, she sees them lying about fat and fatigued in a pile of fresh hay. Curds are strewn about the dirt floor beside their feeding troughs. She asks Claire if she had fed them out. Sheepish and embarrassed, Claire admits her mistake and feels terrible all over again. The thought of how much money has been lost by this simple transgression from the order of things weighs heavily upon Claire's young mind. She takes it seriously and feels heartbroken. It happens, Cat reassures her. There are so many ways to mess up. There are so many variables that can ruin things. Eventually, if something can go wrong, it will.

Elsie and Cat do not often discuss the subject of money in detail, but they will open up their books to any curious intern who shows an interest in the financials of starting and running a small business. It is different for everyone, Cat assures them. It was a different time when we got going here, and everyone's got different needs and wants. There is not one formula out there. You need to discover your formula for your moment in place and time. And hope for more luck than misfortune.

Claire shows some signs of unease around the topic of money. She scrutinizes the numbers on the pages with one eye squinted almost shut. She doesn't want to hold the packet of accounting records in her hands. It is her attempt to avoid knowing how the information contained within them would apply to her situation. Anna is the one who sits down at the desk with an elbow to each side of the documents, interpreting the cash flow from month to quarter to year and the correlations to previous years. The categories are specific at times, easy and direct: grain for goats, vet expenses, delivery expenses, electricity. But in other places it reads: cheese house supplies, which she knows means anything from cultures to cheese wrappers. Paper towels, curd-cutting utensils, or chart recorders for the pasteurizer. It is hard to see the real cost to each batch of cheese. How to calculate the real cost of producing each pound of milk is a mystery even to Cat. Anna scribbles on a scrap piece of paper her own list of things relating to the animals that are absent from the pages, factoring things like the production of five thousand square bales and the land where the goats graze for half the year or more. She wonders how much each doe consumes out there in the wood and pasture. Books in the library tell her four goats per acre, but Elsie's goats prefer the woods to straight grass land.

Claire does not show any interest in Anna's findings and does not probe her about her take on it all. Sustainability for her has never meant profits and capital gains. But Anna sees it tied neatly into the financial reality and necessary monetary decisions. She sees that a creative and practical blend of mind is needed to move any sort of industry forward into health and long lasting success. For Anna, the discovery of making something from nothing and growing it by way of ambition feels liberating and exhilarating.

She pastes the analysis and as much raw data as she can into one of her journals. Recording and saving things that she does not have any present use for is becoming her habit. She has grown accustomed to collecting information of any foreign nature. She had kept attentive and summarized with care everything before her as if the message being conveyed would prove to be of utmost importance. She had scribed it all there like it is a code that will grant her access to some-thing, someday. She isn't sure what, but she is certain that there is something of worth to be copied and absorbed into her journals.

A year now has passed since her time in the woods. The rainy spring is long past, and July is proving to be one of the hottest and driest to which Elsie and Cat ever bore witness. In June, farmers all over the county had scrambled through every stretch of three consecutive dry days to make hay. Cat had grabbed any opportunity he could to mow, tedd, rake, and bale up some dry first cut. On his last attempt, the ten day forecast changed, with nothing in the outlook but dry, hot days. By the time they were done filling the loft with the last wagon loads, they already had started wishing for rain. But to no avail. The wish for dry days from weeks ago had been granted. The second cut would be pushed into August.

Elsie's garden, which everyone swears is the best this season, needs little weeding by the fourth of July. Just watering. Anna lingers there in the garden, trying not to think about this or that. The same way she had looked about the forest floor and the trees she passed on the trail, she lets her mind release from formed sentences and ideas, the constructed thoughts of logic and analysis. No aim, no intention, just awareness about the life around her. The young August-bearing plants amid the fully realized bunches of lettuces, spinach, and beet greens. The diversity of edible delights, all interwoven among the rows, sewed together like quilted strips of cloth, varying shades of green with changing patterns. The flowering plants and adolescent corn stalks feel more like the animals out at pasture, alive with movement and intelligence, at peace with their activity. She hears them munching the sunlight and drawing forth the power to unroot the latent nutrients embedded in the soil. Elsie and she had tilled in a three-year-old compost from one of the goat manure piles early that Spring. The dry earth here in the garden still harbors some of that rich, dark color which is lacking in the grassy land surrounding its edges. Elsie's smile seems to grow even wider when working in the garden with any willing companion. There is something about sharing in the experience of work, outside in the sun and quiet of the landscape. Anna lets her mind drift further now.

Her eyes trace the delicate stems that draw curved lines out of the dirt, the rounded leaves, the small colorful seeds budding, and the vulnerability of everything in front of her. The wind lifts the leaves. Gentle and slow. The movement of these creatures is tied directly to the world around them. What trust it takes. To grow things outside in this world. What hope one must have that everything will be okay in the world. All it takes is one hail storm in late June to wipe out the work, life, and hope in a garden. But all over, in small plots of land and larger ones, people like Elsie tend these delicate creatures with such attention and care. They don't think about what is out of their control. All they can do is love and nurture.

With bunches of greens ready, too much for their kitchens and the farmers market, an opportunity blows in from outside the garden, settling there one afternoon on a Friday. One that would find a home for the excesses of the early harvest and be redeeming for Claire. A great deal of fresh greens, meat, and cheese is needed in Boston before five o'clock for a special event. By word of mouth it comes to them. Claire is the final link to make it all happen. When she told Elsie about it, she felt like she could make up the lost batch of cheese to them. Elsie's first reaction is that it seems suspect. Besides, they don't even know the buyers, how do we know they will pay? Too many small shops and restaurants in the cities use small food producers as banks, holding up payment for months and months. Some go out of business and never pay. Claire explains the situation, and it's even more suspicious once the details are laid out on the table. There is no restaurant. It is not a store. This isn't even a legitimate business. It is an individual who will pay up front in cash upon delivery. What is it all for? Why doesn't she buy it all from specialty food shops in and around Boston? The promised price is quite high. Bigger than the equivalent of three farmers markets. Boston is three hours away, but Claire offers to bring it there. She would spend the night with friends and be back the next day around noon to take over at the farmer's market. Elsie stirs with uneasiness, but she is intrigued and insists on talking to this potential client on the phone. Claire gets her the number. The woman organizing everything in Boston pays her by way of credit card over the phone. Well that's a first, Elsie says. What is she doing, catering an event? A wedding? Claire tells us about this new phenomenon.

Well, it might not be new, I don't know, but it started in Brooklyn. At least, that's where this woman first came across the idea. It's a one night only restaurant.

You see, the location is unknown until an hour before the dinner begins. The only way anyone even knows about it is if they happen to know somebody who invites them along. The thing is, among foodies, it's becoming a topic of conversation. They ask everyone they know to try and get in on one of these events. It's all very illegal. There's an artful quality to the whole thing. Like a play. A wonder if it all will work out. But that's part of the appeal. That and the idea that the restaurant will exist just once. One night, one menu. The production is envisioned and created only once and then gone the next day. An empty quiet space replaces it all. That's what makes it sought after... but what draws them in the first place is that the food is all farm-to-table. Nothing is purchased in stores. All of it directly from farms. Usually trucked in that evening. This woman in particular, she likes to focus on two farms, no more than three, for all the ingredients so as to make the event that much more unique from any previous ones.

How many times has she done one of these?

I'm not sure, but I do know she only puts them on three or four times a year. So once word gets out, those who have been waiting jump on it like its gold and gather a group of friends to go. They always save room for the farmers if they want to attend. For free I mean. They're treated as rock stars at these events.

Have you been to one?

No. But I have friends who have. That's how I got them interested in your farm.

With his hand covering his mouth, Cat listens to it all with amazed delight in his eyes. It is almost hard to believe, he says.

Do you want to go?

No, Cat and Elsie say in unison. I don't think we should be associated with anything illegal, Cat explains his position. I don't know how I feel about it all, Elsie expands. Although a certain part of me, she tells them, loves the fact that these young people want to defy authority with food and make it the center of their party. You two should go in our place, Cat tells them.

It is decided.

Anna heads over to the shed and grabs some baskets for the vegetables and herbs. Elsie goes to the cave. Claire helps her put together an invoice. Within an hour, she and Anna are in her car and en route to Boston.

It's been so long since I've been to the city. What do you want to do?

After, you mean?

We can go out, if you want? Jake lives close to everything.

I don't know.

The car spins along the highway through the southern parts of New Hampshire. Anna stares out at the blur of unknown towns and places. The road seems busier than she remembers it. They follow that stream of vehicles like it's a river sending them forth. Such a fast current, something to which she is not accustomed, having spent so much time in the woods and on the farm.

We haven't stayed up late for a while.

We'll make it happen.

The music fills the space between their words. The old car that Claire drives has a broken antenna, but the CD player works. The disc they play reminds them both that they are young and free of responsibility. The world is open for them to go anywhere. Do anything. So long as they can find the money. She knows it is not the same for everyone, this elated sense of lightness.

I almost got together with Jake. Almost. I could see it happening if we lived in the same place.

What does he do?

He's in management and operations.

What does that mean?

I don't know. I think he consults too.

The outside air blows in through the windows. It is loud, and Anna has to listen actively to hear Claire as she talks about her friend. She wonders at the life of someone like Jake. What does he do when he gets to his job? His routine. Is his work a series of meetings all day, with moments of solitude in between, staring at this screen and then that one? Does he see at the end of the day or the week, or even month by month, the things he has done or made happen? Do they amount to something recognizable such that he can say to himself, there, that is what I have done—there it is.

He worked in India for a while. He might head back there. I don't know.

Claire tells her this quietly. With every mile they gain, edging closer to the city's reach, her tone seems to fade into estrangement. As she gets closer to his location, she realizes what a distance is between them. Anna sees it too.

He does travel to some great places.

Her voice finally gives. She is done. The music changes. Then the car slows. The wind blows more evenly in and out of each window. They don't have to strain to hear one another talk.

Did you call any of those boys from the Long Trail?

No.

Why not? I thought you would.

Too short of a notice. Well...

Who was it again? Darry or Gabe that you camped with?

Anna pauses. Turns slow in the direction of the wind. Drifts and waits.

I would like to do more hikes before leaving this summer.

Gabe? Right? That was the one. Have you heard from him yet? Darry is the one in Boston right?

I don't know.

Claire shifts.

There isn't a lot of space at Jake's. I thought I would share his room. You can have the couch in the hallway living area. Okay?

Sure.

Anna turns back to Claire's face as she tells her this. At the prospect of spending the night with Jake, Claire has allowed her features to grow wide and smile. Anna doesn't disapprove outright, but the age difference between them is enough to make her unsupportive. Jake is almost thirty years old. Claire is twenty-one. Anna too had played with the idea of dating older boys but found that the maturity she was attracted to in them had replaced or negated some other more important character trait. She couldn't pinpoint what it was. But it was missing.

Jake is excited about the event. He is bringing some of the guys from his work along. It should be fun.

Their conversation continues like this. Claire's daydreams of the hours to come. Anna's mind trying to find her place in it all. What her role will be. It has been some time since she was in the circumstances of the city. Who are these people that are coming to dinner?

The fast drive on the highway is something like a memory from a past self she almost remembers.

When they reach the real traffic flows around Boston, Anna looks out her window at the opposing cars and thinks to herself how peculiar she feels in comparison to all of them. A seemingly endless line of millions of people pass by her open window and wear expressions on their faces that are not intended for her to interpret. She and Claire are strangers to them all. It also must have been in Claire's thoughts at the same moment. In the midst of a climactic intersection of Boston's veins of traffic, the dizzying array of countless vehicles, Claire turns to Anna and wonders out loud about how—somewhere in this maze of cars—some of these people could have eaten the cheese they had made back at the farm. Some of them could be heading to a restaurant with friends right now and will be ordering an appetizer with the farm's name in the description on the menu. Claire's thought brings Anna closer to the whole experience, and, despite its mystical romanticism, Anna feels there is truth in it.

Just as they reach their destination, Anna changes her response to one of Claire's earlier inquiries. They have driven to where the woman told them to park, pulled right up to the spot, turned off the car, and started to open their doors when Anna clarifies it for her.

Well I did send an email.

Huh?

To Darry. I don't have the others' emails.

Did he write back?

I don't know. We had to leave, so I just left it open. I gave him all the information and the location.

What does he do?

I don't remember. I think he studied economics.

The woman is there to greet them. She is waiting outside of the building, shifting her focus between their arrival and pressing her thumbs into the device in her hand. She is dressed like one would expect of a woman in a city preparing for a special event: mostly dark blacks with a couple spots of subtly colored patterns. Claire and Anna had not considered what they were wearing until that moment. Freeing up one hand to greet them, her eyes continue to shift back and forth from them to her other preoccupied hand.

Thank you so much for doing this. We're thrilled you're participating.

I'm Anna.

I'm Claire.

My name is Yolanda. It is so good to meet both of you. I feel like a bit of the farm is still present on your aura.

She gives her complete attention to them as she speaks with a focused and sincere smile about her features. It lasts only a brief moment or two, but the act of noticing and making conversation is in direct contrast to the way strangers speak to one another in rural parts.

The next hours are spent in rapid preparation. They play their part in the effort. Anna shows the chef her technique for cutting the big wheels of cheese and the best methods for presentation. Every cheese demands a different approach to revealing its innards so as to be devoured. Anna takes this seriously, as so much had gone into the production. She had brought those animals to specific grasses, taken care in both the milking and the handling of those curds, watched their ripening over months in the aging room, and brought the finished cheeses here to this city in this moment. The last act of creation was this: its cut.

Claire helps with the herbs they have brought from Elsie's garden. The chef wants them washed and ready to eat fresh as the guests' appetites desire. They are placed in hand-made pottery pieces and displayed like floral arrangements, but with the very real intention of their being taken out and placed in salads, soup, and other dishes. Claire also carries the knowledge of the food's history as she works. She had watched over them as seeds in her apartment, watered them daily, transplanted them outdoors when ready, and harvested them just earlier that day after Yolanda had ordered them.

The space Yolanda has chosen for the event requires some improvisation, but finally it is ready to accomplish its purpose. The creative workings of the kitchen and placement of the tables among the eccentricities of this old building all add up to something incredible, Anna decides. She feels the city. It is just outside these walls, but the farms of Vermont are inside. It does not seem to be a dichotomy, but a harmony. She will know for sure soon enough. When the doors open with a gust of people, then Anna's work at the farm will be complete. Her acts of creation will be consummated in the slow rhythmic motions of the diner's mouths. The destruction of the myriad hues and forms of the food bearing new life with the tender rendering of each flavor and texture.

It is not like her meals alone in the woods.

The room fills with the sounds of a hundred conversations.

Do you make the cheese?

Yes.

How many times a day do you have to milk a goat?

The same as a cow. Twice a day.

How do you make cheese?

She pauses. This is a question that Cat would answer in his usual cerebral manner. The process is a combination of science and art. Its variables both controlled by laboratorial methods and directed by imagination and intuition to make something unique. There are two main categories, fresh and semi-aged cheeses in one and harder, firm cheeses in the other. The latter one, you begin with milk at... Elsie would interrupt and try to rein him in. Anna tries at it with Elsie in mind.

You take fresh milk and sour it by adding culture. Then you add rennet to coagulate the milk solids and separate the whey. Once it has begun to set, you can do a variety of things depending on what you are making. You can cut the curds first if you are not making a soft cheese. You can even warm up the curds. Pour them into moulds to give them shape. Then press them or not. Then salt or brine them. Then age them. That is the gist of it.

As the people arrive and mingle in crowds around tables filled with cheeses, breads, and vegetables, Anna and Claire notice that the conversations all are directed at them and the other farmers in the room. A barrage of question after question about life on the farm. About cheese. About why they are doing the internship.

The people around Anna are talking much more than she is. They leave little room for her to speak. Just as she begins to answer, she is interrupted and asked another question. But before she can reset, the guests will speculate numerous answers and related stories of their own. Overall, the spectrum of sound and velocity of dialogue make for a turbulent and scattered experience.

This world teems with others.

There are seemingly endless possibilities for conversation. Distinct stories to learn. Different perspectives. New paradigms. She sees Claire in her periphery, standing on one side of the room with three young men dressed in tight fitting city clothes. She doesn't recognize them. None of them are familiar from the photos Claire has shared with her. She notices Claire has a natural ability to flirt in a quiet yet effective manner. The couple standing next to Anna are from the city. They have bought the farm's cheese for years now. They have seen pictures of Cat and Elsie at one of the stores they frequent, but this is the closest they have come to putting a live face to the product they love. Anna receives all the accolades and praise as if it were her farm and her creation alone. They give her the credit since she is there now, representing the cheese. Anna stares at them, wondering who it is she has become.

Anna is not the person she will be years from now, but times like these seem to disregard the order of things, the past, present and future. She mingles with her later self in this moment, and I know her. The memory resides as a story I can retell, a narrative with detail from a specific point in time, yet the feelings and their meaning grasped and attributed later. In this way the memory lays root in my eternal self.

I know her now, as she stands chatting with one eye on the couple in front of her and the other grabbing hold of something unexpected. A figure walking in from the outside. At first I don't know him, but something pulls me back to look again. My body reacts and turns to discern his face. I do know who that is. I excuse myself and start to move in his direction. But just as quickly as I have aimed myself at him, I slow. I regain my composure and watch him as I edge closer. His hair is the same, and the look on his face is the same. He meanders between individuals as if they are trees that he needs to avoid as he hikes along. No one is with him, but I can see he is seeking someone. He doesn't make it obvious. Not turning this way and that, only his eyes move to scan the people around him quietly. That is his way after all. Once my footpath homes in and matches his, I lock my vision hard on him. He sees me now too.

You two met on the trail hiking?

Yes.

How?

At the table, we tell the story of our meeting that early morning in the quiet of the forest. The recounting of this event feels strange, and I can see that Gabe is uneasy about dramatizing it for these urban strangers, so far from the privacy of that pathway in the woods. As more questions come about our time together on the trail, an allusion swims about the conversation that perhaps our relationship is something more than either of us have ever considered. It is by way of these musings from others that something is becoming apparent, whether we like it or not. Gabe looks at me. His gaze is straight on. He doesn't look away, and his expression is undefinable.

So why had you decided to hike the Long Trail?

I hadn't decided I was. I didn't know how far I would go. I didn't actually hike all of it.

Gabe's answer is more or less the same, but he does note more specifically why he had been out there. He tells a story about his childhood and how much he had loved the woods near his home. He never really had found anything since then that brought him so close to feeling alive and like himself. So, being able to choose what he wanted to do for the first time in life, he went to the very mountains that he had been staring at in the distance the whole while he had been studying in college.

Why do most people hike it do you think?

Most of the people I had encountered were not doing it with a specific goal, like a pilgrimage. It was more about being alone in nature. Being physical and away from modernity. Communing with this country of ours in a more intimate way. Maybe even feeling the wildness about the human condition. I do not speak any of these reasons aloud, not in those words at least. Darry and Rich did it to say they had, or maybe because they felt it would make them well-rounded before merging completely into city life. I did it because I love the mountains. And if I had to guess and answer for Gabe—well, I think he was there because he is a seeker.

Gabe answers in a way that doesn't directly address the question. Someone once told me that in becoming a creative individual, twenty percent of one's focus should be on the work of others. The other eighty percent is looking at nature.

There are plenty of young people around the table who I can tell do not understand at all. I can see their minds trying to grasp at this. For a couple of them, I can read it on their faces, the world they inhabit both physically and in their imaginations is singularly urban and diversified only by the landscapes of other cities they may have visited over their lives. Their connection with organic farming manifests in small community gardens in cities, in the potted gardens outside their apartment windows. Some of them are quite experienced at growing vegetables in these carved out spaces. One of them even cures his own meats in an old, miniature fridge occupying his one bedroom apartment. His girlfriend winces. She confesses that it scares her a little every time they peer in to see what is growing. A certain quality to his telling signals that he regards the act of aging meats as subversive. As if this dinner event is trifling compared to the unregulated growing activities back home in his apartment.

Gabe listens to everyone talk around him, and it seems that he doesn't quite fit into any group represented there that evening. What

I mean is, Gabe could become a part of anything. This was something I had begun to decipher when camping with him, but now, out of that context and in what some consider a more real place, I can see it plainly. For the rest of the night, Gabe and I wander the room together, sitting in one place with some people, standing on the other side of the room with others, but always together. As we talk and meet new people, I realize that this paradox about him and his relationship to others is his defining character trait.

Gabe and I, along with Claire and Jake, are talking to a large group of people while eating dessert. The conversation centers on the question of why one would intern at a farm. This had come up with nearly every group of strangers we met that night. Three other young women in the group also had interned at farms throughout all parts of the northeast.

Do these places only hire women?

I have met a few guys, but most of them are there because of a girlfriend or soon-to-be wife.

The farm I worked at said that one hundred percent of their applicants are women some years. Most of the time they're lucky to get one guy applicant.

One of the young women would be better described as a girl. She is just about to turn eighteen and had interned the past two summers at three different farms. One in Pennsylvania and two in upstate New York. Later I learn that she couldn't stand being at her parents' house anymore and had lived at these farms all summer. She had attended boarding school and was eagerly looking forward to college. Perhaps she was looking for a surrogate family, but, in the end, these family farms also had proved a disappointment for her on the home-front level.

One of the farms I stayed at, the husband left his wife for one of the interns. She was twenty-three, and he was close to forty.

The farming world has its own rumor mill. Claire and I had heard of numerous family farms where the family designation had to be stripped away. This isn't the first time we have heard of such a story. What makes it so upsetting, why it is so difficult to swallow, is that these interns had been invited into the family to a certain extent. It seems such a horrible betrayal.

I could see how that could happen.

Claire shudders, and her expression darkens. Had Jake really just said that? I can see the tension building around her eyes and her difficulty in processing what her almost boyfriend had just suggested. Then someone counters, perhaps on her behalf.

What do you mean? Because they are working so closely together?

No. I just think it is bound to happen. And I think it happens in all sorts of places. When I have been oversees, consulting in various industries, I see it all the time.

I watch Claire. She cannot help but think that Jake's indifferent and easy tone about the whole affair is alarming. She had met Jake as an intern at her last job. He was not exactly her boss, but he had been a colleague of her boss. I intervene to help re-direct the conversation.

Well, at the farm where Claire and I live, I can assure you that Elsie and Cat are more than devoted to one another. They are deeply bonded to each other in a way that is clear to anyone who spends anytime whatsoever there. And besides, do we really want to get to know our products this intimately? Must we really know everything about what we consume? Do we need to know what the conversation was between two people as they picked our Swiss chard and kale?

Gabe turns to one of the other women. She goes by the name Star. He sees what I am trying to do and helps guide the conversation firmly out of where it had been. Star has been working all summer for two sisters in their fifties, who made over twenty-thousand square bales of hay a year. She had mentioned it earlier, and Gabe was fascinated to hear more.

I have always wanted to mow a field of hay.

It's more than just that you know.

I'm sorry. That probably sounded very naïve.

Despite Star's eccentric name, she is a solid looking individual. She too stands tall like Anna, with strong limbs and a rough quality to her physique. Her hands alone distinguish her from the rest of the women and men in the room. They are taut and covered with bulging veins. It was as if the whole of her hand is one big callous. Being stroked by such a hand would feel like sandpaper. The other intern by contrast is short with a silky smooth quality to her, the definition of feminine. She too has been working with Star at the hay farm and had surprised the whole team of hay unloaders with her ability to carry two forty-pound bales at a time across the hay loft.

I know it sounds strange, but I have always felt drawn to hay fields. I don't know why. I'm sure the women you work for would laugh at me saying so.

No. I think so long as you made an effort to help move bales around, they would completely respect you. They probably won't let you mow a field though. I haven't seen them let anyone else run the mower or the baler, or even the rake. When they get really busy, they might set someone up with the tedder on the tractor. But that's easy compared to the rest of it.

Star's companion speaks up at this point, but her voice matches her small frame and smooth delicate features. Her quiet voice compels everyone lean in to hear her speak. She does not fight against the crowd's amplifying tones, or even try and compete to be heard. Clearly, she is a stranger to such scenes with loud throngs of people.

You should come and stay at the farm for a few days. We're about to do third cut. There isn't as much hay to unload like in June with first cut, but they would still appreciate the help. They start getting tired in September.

She looks at Gabe and delivers the invitation in such a way that evokes an unmistakable feeling in me. It is the first time I have been with Gabe around other women our age, pretty women. I realize that I had been with Gabe only in the context of other boys. Gabe seems unaware of any hidden motives. Probably none of the others in our group pick up on it, save Star, since she knows this girl well. The thing is, I didn't expect this feeling to show up in me. I can't remember the last time even a pinch of jealousy got in me. If it had been Star that asked him, I wonder, would I still be feeling this way? Star resembles me, but something about this other girl doesn't seem right for Gabe. She isn't for him, I decide, with a judicious reasoning governing my thoughts.

Where is the farm? Is it far from here?

No. It is near the border of Massachusetts, Vermont, and New York.

Gabe nods his head slowly as she speaks. He almost inquires more about the farm but then leans his head back just slightly and closes his lips together. I can tell what he is doing. He opens himself up to others, sometimes in the subtlest of ways, and they are attracted to him. Just as their interest in getting closer to him widens though, he draws back into a more aloof persona. Not because he intentionally wants to guard himself from others, he doesn't even seem aware of what he is doing.

I'll think about it. Thanks for the reference to their farm.

His cordial tone settles the situation. For now. I look over to him, taking my eyes off the other girl's gaze in his direction. I would not characterize my sudden pinch of jealousy as something that could be read on my face. In truth, I never would have admitted the feeling to anyone and would have acted the opposite if I suspected someone had detected it. But it was there, however small. I felt it, and that was all that mattered. I know something is behind that pang, even though I am not willing to face it at this moment.

The conversation around us has moved away from making hay, from affairs, and from interns and farms. The group starts talking more generally about being in their twenties, about our generation of young people living both in and out of cities. Nothing specific anymore. Just speculation about the big picture of everything that is going on in our lives. Jake has a lot to say, and Gabe counters him, recalling for me the conversations that he and Darry would have. Claire listens but doesn't add anything. She looks with frustration at Jake, but he doesn't react at all to her posture and glare. He doesn't seem to care this way or that how anyone feels. But later, when the event concludes and we walk down the streets of Boston, slowly making our way with him and Gabe back to his apartment, he puts his arm around her side and pulls her close to him. He gives her one quick look, and, in that flash of an instant, he has her back. She would spend the night in his room. I would be alone on the couch in the hallway.

Gabe. What do you want to do…

I don't finish my question right away. I am tired, and it is unclear when we might see each other again. The room is almost dark. We can hear muffled talking through the door to the bedroom. I had posed the question ambiguously but can't quite figure how to phrase what I want to ask him. Life takes on a new meaning for me in this moment. I forget how old I am. I forget that I don't really know much about Gabe's past. But some quality about him gives me the feeling that he is one of my oldest friends.

I want to learn how to make hay.

Is that it?

I don't know what exactly it is I should do.

What about your art?

I know I will do that. But I need to do something practical. Something that is needed. Or at least, where I can see the definite need... I'm not even sure that makes any sense.

Cat says things like that all the time, but really I think that what he needs is something more than what is needed. He seems to want to have both. The practical, making food, which is such a basic need. And also the philosophical, connection, meaning, the making sense of it all.

Don't misunderstand me. I don't have any illusions of grandeur about changing the world. I just want to carve out my own little spot. Root myself there. Live as honestly as possible. Make a beautiful world that exists as an opportunity to change the world, should others pass through it. Each visitor will be reminded of what it is about life that is worth living. Not as something imposing or even fully realized, but as something that is always growing and becoming new.

A farm?

Yes, a farm.

The significance of what Gabe would say next could be overlooked by anyone except us. It would be said with complete and casual honesty, as anything ordinary might be said between us. Sometimes unexpected things come forth into the present from some other time in himself. This was not the most unexpected, but it changed the course of time for us that night. It advanced us to some other time in our life, or took us out of time all together.

I think starting a farm would be the most creative thing. We could make something…

That is it. The part where he includes both of us into his vision. It had been a recurring joke between us, how he only spoke in the first person singular. And now, the time I hear him jump grammatically into the plural, it is not about us going here or there, or this small thing or that one. It is about the whole trajectory of our life. And still, it feels normal. It was said easily, because it was the most clear thing to both of us. I let it enter my thoughts the same way I breathe my next breath, without being conscious of it.

The rest of the night we talk about our ideas for a farm that we would create. It is the kind of naïve conversation that Cat would have put his blessing to, telling us how necessary such a thing is for any new and great thing ever to come to being. It is always with the naïve where the imagination can feel free to create what is needed.

That night I do not sleep alone as I had previously concluded that I would. Again, Gabe and I find ourselves in a new place, sharing sleep together. As we lie side by side on the floor next to Jake's couch, we again feel a deep familiarity with each other. The way he shuffles his feet just before falling asleep, the smell of his bare shoulder and the hushed breathing that comes from his lips only inches from my own. None of it makes us nervous the way we should have felt, having never kissed. We have moved past all of that, reached to the end of ourselves and come head on with something much bigger than the physical consummations in companionship. Within seconds we are asleep, our hearts not beating fast with anticipation but slowly and at peace in the feeling that everything is right and in its place.

Build therefore your own world. As fast as you conform your life to the pure idea in your mind, that will unfold its great proportions.

—Emerson, *Nature*

E very so often this happens. I approach my daily tasks and find myself thinking: what am I doing all this for? But I don't get lost in that thought. It arises but does not demand a response. I recognize this as the onset of a period of time that I call an age of critical questions. The questions will grow subtly more persistent and inhabit all the conversations I undertake. It will color my actions, my relationships until it becomes my identity to a degree. I know that I will leave this place and set about the tasks necessary to accomplish my dreams. Ideas and goals arise from these questions, and I will go about making them manifest into reality. This period is an age of struggle. The big picture will be framed. Passion, intuition, and will power are my means of survival and blaze a path to what it is I am after. Then, unannounced, a third period of time in this cycle will arrive. It is the most elusive and rather perplexing. I don't know what to name it. But now, I am here in a place I imagined all those years ago. I have built upon the rolling green canvas of earth outside my window. It appears from all angles that my original dream has been solidified, yet I am again in that age of critical questions. What have I done all this for?

Gabe watches Cat in the early October light standing over his New Holland square baler, wrestling with the large fly wheel at the end of the PTO shaft. He turns the wheel with his hands, but seems to be drawing the power he needs from all parts of his body, including the words coming out of his lips. It is difficult to find what keeps causing the fly wheel's bolt to break and shut down all the other parts of this complex machine. The teeth that swipe along the ground, snatching up the hay and tossing it up into the large mouth of the machine. The steel plunger which then punches and compacts the hay into its square shape. The intricate weaving of twine around the bale until the knots are tied. The final spinning parts lead the finished bale to a fast moving conveyor that ejects the bale twenty feet into the air like some heroic catapult of farming triumph. All of this depends on that fly wheel shear bolt. And yet, when the bolt snaps in two, it is a sacrifice much appreciated by all the other parts. They don't suffer any serious harm as a result of the machine coming to a complete and sudden halt. Cat explains this all to Gabe, stopping only to catch his breath or jump back to the bigger picture of what critical questions he is facing at this point in his life.

You know, about fifteen years ago, a friend asked me how the haying was going that summer. This is a question I am asked every summer, by other haymakers as well as people who know little about it. But for some reason, that day, all I could mutter about this whole enterprise, was that it's shit, it's just… shit.

Gabe waits for the next part to this story, but Cat doesn't say anything else. He watches as Cat turns the fly wheel one last time, hearing the slip clutch click into place and making sure all the parts move as they should. Instead of continuing his thoughts about haymaking, Cat says instead, well, let's see if it works this time. We've only got three more bolts left, I'm running low. Let's hope whatever it was, it's done messing with us for now. Then, he hops back on to the tractor, turns on the engine, and pushes the acceleration throttle to 540 rpms. He engages the PTO, looking back the whole while as the baler comes back to life. The flywheel immediately spins and sets the entire machine into motion. At first, the sound is an awful cacophony, a violent clanging of steel. But it soon assumes a rhythmic structure, a patterned ensemble of perfectly timed movements.

The melody is bearable only because it signals to the keen ear that everything is as it should be. For now, it is not shit.

It takes about ten more minutes for Cat to fill up the wagon. A wave of his hands communicates to Gabe over the impossible decibels that he should take the wagon load back to the barn, unload it and bring it back as soon as he can. He hadn't instructed Gabe before starting up the baler again, probably because he didn't want to assume the problem was fixed until he was sure that it had been. Twenty minutes ago, Cat's mind was probably thinking that all the wind rows of hay out there might not be picked up that day and would be spoiled tomorrow by the forecasts calling for an early rain. Now, his mind was singularly trained on getting all that hay unloaded before the sun set and the night's dew started settling.

Anna is still up in the hay loft, shifting around bales and stacking the older ones six or seven feet high to make room for this late autumn harvest of third and some rare fourth cut. She peeks her head out of the hay loft's window, where the bales enter from the hay elevator and meet up with the conveyor perched high up by the ceiling of the barn. She is bent over because there is not enough distance from the conveyor to the ceiling to stand up straight. She had heard the tractor coming and climbed up there to get ready for the bales. She would push them off at the one spot in the long, one hundred and twenty foot loft that still had room for more hay. It is not as hot up there as it had been in June, July, and August. The air is cleaner and cooler, and she even wears long sleeves as she works. Gabe parks the tractor, hops off in a flash, and sets on pulling bales out of the wagon's side and sending them up the conveyors to Anna. He moves with urgency and with an energy that she has never before seen in him. He grabs at the bales and pulls at the twine, his forearms in a constant state of flex. Even from her high perch, Anna can observe all of this. He gets the wagon unloaded as fast as Cat or any other experienced farmer would have, and then he takes the tractor back to the field where Cat is finishing up with another wagon load. The wheels are in motion. They all move about their tasks engaged in that rhythm together but alone in their individual parts of the process.

While Anna waits for the next load of hay to arrive, she sits for a moment on the conveyor in the loft, looking down at the finished stacks and the pile waiting to be stacked. The afternoon light shines between the clapboards of the barn, making beautiful and strange, almost mystical, contrasts of dark and light. The whole illuminated scene and perspective from where she sits is like no other place she has ever been. It is so unlike rooms in houses or even the view from standing in other parts of the barn. Up there, at the very top of this thirty foot barn, in this massive space where thousands of bales keep in the dark, she feels connected to all the other boys, girls, men or women over the years who also had observed this view. She imagines some woman her age from the past, maybe sixty or seventy years ago, sitting up there, taking a rest for a moment, and seeing the thousands of horizontal lines of light breaking through the clapboards. What had she thought about up here? Who was she? The moment resembles only a handful of moments in her life. Moments like sitting alone on the top of a mountain. Or sitting in some foreign country's cathedral, listening to the indecipherable words harmonically echoing through the majestic architecture. She looks about the loft's space, memorizing all of it, and then jumps down about seven or eight feet onto the soft landing of a firmly stacked group of bales. She sets back into motion, lifting and placing each bale as it should be. Why is it that some physical tasks, more than others, bring her to the very root of being alive? How is it that she finds transcendence in the simplicity and ardor of stacking bales? Would this feeling last year after year, after one hundred thousand bales have been stacked? Two hundred thousand, a quarter million?

Gabe appears at the loft's ladder entrance from below. He finishes stacking with Anna and offers to switch jobs. She doesn't want to at first.

I feel like I need to see this out to the end up here.

Are you sure? It is really nice outside in the sun. I can barely see in here right now, I don't know how you see anything.

No. I can't stop. This loft has been mine all summer during haying.

I understand. And it is so close to being done. I think Cat only has one more load after this one, probably only a half load.

I feel like seeing all of these thousands of bales packed in here helps me to see something in myself. Don't ask me what. But it is satisfying to look at.

Alright, yell down to me when you get up there and you're ready.

Gabe disappears back down ladder.

The daylight seems perfectly timed to Cat's arrival with the final wagon of hay. Just as the last bales are sent up the elevator, the cool air brings a chill to each of them, and the light disappears. Anna exits the hay loft's window at the very peak of the barn and climbs onto the top of the hay elevator. To her, it doesn't seem that dark, considering where she had just been, and she secures herself on the side rail before sliding down to the ground like a teenager might do. She smiles as she stretches her body straight and tall and then jogs over to where Cat and Gabe are talking with Elsie. They are invited into the main house for dinner and some well-earned beers. The kitchen feels like a real home to both Anna and Gabe, and Cat and Elsie seem like a combination of parental figures and older siblings. Something in between perhaps, but definitely familial. The room is filled with the warm smells of at least six or seven different things cooking from the garden. As Anna begins talking with Elsie about what spices are in one of the dishes, she catches a glimpse of Gabe looking at her. His gaze is unwavering, almost intense, but only because it is a revealing stare, one that communicates so much between the two of them. No conversation could equate to the vast amount of information crossing the room at the speed of light into the dilation of each other's pupils. Was it something about this room, with these figures before them setting the table, with food after the hard work on their land? What was the reason for this being an epiphanic moment? It is, after all, nothing extraordinary. But in the ordinary, in the actual, she finds real insight waiting in plain sight.

Later that night, after a long and easy conversation around the table and once Anna and Gabe are alone again in the intern apartment, another slip in time reveals itself. As if from the mouth of a sixty- or seventy-year-old Gabe, somehow mixed up with the present Gabe, a phrase is uttered mistakenly that to this day still seems unreal and unbelievable. No amount of persuasion would convince the listeners of this story to the truth of it. From their attunement, it steps out of some eternal realm into the naked truth and comes face to face with the obvious, the undeniable, the heart of the matter. It had begun with a question at dinner. A shallow well of tears had formed around Anna's eyes. Nothing drastic, not streaming out onto her cheeks, but a watery glaze coated her vision for a couple of minutes as the conversation rolled around stories of their pasts, their childhoods. They all had talked of their mothers, and that had done it for her.

Tell me something about your mother. If you had to tell me just one thing about her.

Anna thinks for a moment, but it doesn't take long for her to realize the perfect thing to say.

Every summer my mother has her gardens. Vegetables and flowers. But the thing about my mother, if I had to share just one detail about her, is the flower arrangements she makes. It wasn't until I got older that I really understood not only how extraordinary the arrangements are, but how the very act of her making them is so creative and inspiring. I kept telling myself that I should be photographing them, as there really is an expression there just as much as in a painting or a sculpture. It's difficult to really make the point of how unique her arrangements are and unlike something you would see in a flower shop. She limits herself and seems to capture a single feeling in these arrangements. Not overusing colors or aiming just to be as bright and pretty as possible. She is more subtle, like an artist, working instinctively and deliberately on the lines that the stems draw, the heights, the overall shapes, and how the compositions and colors relate to the unique vases she chooses. She seems to listen to what the flowers want and seeks to make them be seen, out of the context of the landscape. She allows them to stand still and triumphantly within the confines of the interior world, for us to live with their truth and beauty as we go about our lives in our homes. They are like still life paintings, a blend of the conceptual and the beautiful. That is the best way to describe them. And then they are gone. She never seems concerned about the permanency of her art, and I'm not sure if she even realizes it is her art. But I remember them, and I appreciate them when they are in her home.

Gabe listens to her without the slightest suggestion that he might interrupt at any point.

After, upon entering their apartment, their private space, a seemingly innocent and natural hug brings Anna and Gabe into a more unexpected feeling. Anna revisits the emotions that had been welling up inside her during dinner. Gabe can feel this and squeezes her, cupping the back of her head in one of his hands. Without thinking, he says aloud words that he had not thought out and perhaps is not even conscious of as he speaks them. What comes out of his mouth is not what he intends to say. What he thinks he is saying, the small part of his mind that is in control of his speech at that moment, is a kind and genuine phrase: I am so glad that you are in my life. But that is not what he actually says. Perhaps because he has lost control of his ability to decipher his feelings or plan his words, he allows a different word to replace the intended word and somehow, somehow the sentence still sounds like it is meant for her and from him. What is said is this: I am so glad you are my wife.

She pulls back, but not abruptly. She keeps her arms around him and looks at him as a slow, revealing smile transpires her lips. She knows he is a serious kid. She knows that he is different than other boys, but this slip seems too comical for his nature. The boy who seems capable of just disappearing without a word or a goodbye. This young man, who guards his heart from being touched by others despite the way he keeps it open for others to read, finds himself transcending all of that and proves how full of utter contradiction he is. He has become her companion. What that means, well that is being defined with each unfolding scene between them. But now, these mistaken words in this slip of time are the first revelation about what their companionship is. He corrects himself, telling her what he meant to say, and truly looks bewildered as to what has just come out of his mouth. Her smile turns into a laugh, and she pulls him back into her arms to hug him this time. All the sadness she had felt during and after dinner has been lifted from the evening. Her reaction to the statement would always remain the same. It somehow didn't seem like a mistake, and there was nothing even slightly strange about it. If anything, the only oddity to it all was that she didn't feel strange about the slip of words.

Over the next two weeks, they never speak about that night. It isn't necessary. In the slow churning of his mind, Gabe finally grasps what it is that perhaps had led him to say those words. Again, during a dinner that they share just the two of them, a recipe that he had acquired from his grandmother, they find their conversation drifting away from the present, which is where their relationship has always kept them. Their dreams and thoughts circle back to past events and spin forward to the people they hope to become. It is here that Gabe has another thought, but this time it is well thought out. He seems to be very certain about it. And again, it contains an enormity of strangeness, almost purposely out of time and place yet again. But he knows it this time. It is as if he has a direct line with his future self and is able to channel his own future thoughts. At the very least, he is looking out for his future self, his forty-year-old self, even his eighty-year-old self. It is not a logic that guides him though. It is pure heart and instinct. In fact, if logic ever had been present in him, he probably never would have found his way into the woods many seasons ago and into her company in the first place. It certainly would not have led him to this farm, this apartment, and this close to her tonight. It is his intuition that is growing into a real power, propelling him into situations of friendship and direction.

You know, I think you would be an incredible mother.

What?

I mean it. I cannot think of anyone I have ever met or imagined who I would want to be the mother of my kids, until now. I know it sounds crazy to say, but I mean it. I just know it about you.

Anna says nothing. She just looks at Gabe as she sits on the couch. She sets down her glass. She processes what he is saying, realizing that he himself doesn't know what a tremendous statement this is. He had spoken deliberately, but his naïve boyishness does not fully understand the enormity of saying something like this, at least not the way she does. How is it that his instincts are so strong and so set upon her to conjure up this declaration? How is it that they share a dwelling? How is it that life has given him every opportunity to see her in such a light, and still he cannot set his desire on her? What is it that shades this part of his heart from her? She watches him say this with that rare, sweet blend of young seriousness and childlike purity and can't help but feel the weight of such a compliment. Anna comes face to face with this statement, while Gabe's vision is set upon something distant and out of time and place as usual.

This is the moment of critical questions Cat had talked of. The world would be imagined in the pure minds of this young Anna and this young Gabe. And all the future selves of each would build and inhabit their creation, would inherit the lives given to them by these two freshly formed minds and fledgling hearts. His statement ushers her to that precipice where all these future moments come into view. There, on the mountain's clearing, she feels a tingle of vertigo, beholding the expanse of life's possibilities and trajectories that now have materialized into focus before her.

In each moment of life, wherever she finds herself, there are the same ten individuals. The older she gets, the easier it is to know who these ten are. It has become expected that she will find these characters. When she arrives at a new place in her life, she always finds one right off, whether she realizes it at that moment or not. The rest present themselves over time. She sees them coming from amidst the crowd and can pick most of them out easily. Some of the roles they play are immutable, and she merely switches a name from a past place with a new one. Some replace former names altogether, assuming new roles as her life changes. One or two are always elusive and may not even be named. They do not show themselves readily, but their being hard to pin down does not mean that they are somehow more or less closely connected to her heart. They may play only a small part in her life. They may only show up for a brief moment once a year even, but they can be counted as being of the ten. She marks these people in her mind and is continually amazed at how this never seems to end. Of the ten however, only one occupies the primary locus of her time and affection. That one she most certainly names and grants all the designations he or she rightly deserves.

When Gabe wandered onto her path that one early morning, none of her persons occupied her space. She was alone, and the ten were present only within herself, where they always had been in the first place. Gabe wandered out as if born from her imagination, without her approval. An escaped soul from the artistic workings of her studio, a Galatea from her Pygmalion sculptures, a tiny craftwork of wood and leaf and grasses, set free and hiding in the wild. He came from there perhaps. And now, he manifests in the form of one of the ten. She lived with just the one for a time, until others arrived and occupied their rightful spots in her domain. And then, they disappeared, and she found others who were marked for that intimate number of souls. Who was she to him though? Which one of the ten did she represent for Gabe? For Claire? For the Norwegian woman who so clearly seemed to be a relation of hers? She must be the one to Gabe, she decides, and he to her. The peculiar thing about their relationship, to which she finally becomes conscious, is that they had from the start spent the night side by side. At first tent by tent, but close enough for the intimacies of sleep and waking to be a part of their life from the start. The bed they shared at the inn along the trail, the couch together in Jake's apartment. And here they are again, continuing their stay with one another, sharing a small apartment together. Before Claire had left, the two twin beds were apart and a tapestry hung between them to symbolize some kind of privacy. Now, with Gabe having replaced her at the farm, the beds are adjacent to one another with nothing hanging between them. She realizes they have never dated, not in the usual sense. Not even once have they resembled two individuals who consider a night or day spent together as a date. What does this mean for them? What does it mean that the thing growing between them has been arranged by forces out of their control?

Cat had mentioned once to her and Claire that it was important not to attempt the fruitless search, like so many of their age, of trying to "find one's self." Instead, he implored them, start the real purpose of life, which is "to create one's self." He said that it was not his own great idea. He had clarified this thought from books, as with the thoughts behind so many of his utterances. It rested unformed in his brain, and he did not come to the real understanding of it until it was revealed in someone else's writing long ago. He himself had created his life, just as Elsie had hers. The real luck of the whole thing was that the two of them were equally committed to their creations, and that they had partnered so well in realizing them.

This time on the farm, she knows, is an interval of sorts. Like college had been. Just as the time she spent in the woods. She carries no illusions about what the next phase of life would entail. It would arise like the crest of a ridgeline, emerging from shade to light, from hidden to revealed, from protected to exposed. It would appear as a wider world in the distance, in such stark contrast as to make her old world seem small and introverted. The act of reaching this next phase mostly would be work. Often tedious. Often lonely. It may be misunderstood by others. But above all, in creating her self and her life, the most difficult aspect would be the formation of identity that inevitably is entangled with doing. Cat is the reluctant cheesemaker. At first unable to accept the label, but that is who he is. Elsie, the farmer. Less reluctant perhaps, but still she must come to terms with that definition as her purpose day in and day out. That is her. So many, Cat warns, are unable to create a self only because of this: the fear of limiting the self, by choosing this over that. In not choosing, they imagine that they will "find" their identities, and those identities will manifest all of their dreams, the limitless definitions of who they are, and what they desire out of life. Don't do that, Cat tells us. Create.

But don't you worry about not succeeding? Or things changing? Or being wrong?

No. Well, maybe I did in the beginning. Yes, I definitely did have those worries. All the time. But they don't compare at all to the later worries, the ones that come to you once you have succeeded.

Like things changing after that?

No. Not exactly. I'll tell you, the thing that plagues me the most is all of the responsibility that comes along with making a product, with taking care of employees, with every critical logistical aspect of our business. These are the things I never expected many years ago when Elsie and I set out to create a farm.

But someone has to take on those responsibilities. You can't just throw up your hands and live in a world where you are afraid to do those things. It seems that they would come naturally after you've been empowered by success.

You sound like Elsie, you know. That is what she always says to reassure me. But the truth is, sometimes I just don't feel worthy of accepting the title of cheesemaker. Now, I'm not saying that to get attention or to have you try and change my mind about it. I say it because this is what happens so often to people who get to a certain point in their careers. They feel like frauds... and if someone doesn't feel like a fraud, well then maybe they are one.

What are you talking about? You're telling us to go and create ourselves, go boldly and passionately in whatever direction we decide. But then, after we've succeeded, we should stop and say that we're frauds after all?

Exactly.

Anna can see that he does not mean it, not entirely. But she also can tell that these are new thoughts, not fully realized in him. He is working them out and trying to come to some agreement with himself on what it all meant. She doesn't agree with his assertion, although Gabe seems intrigued by it. Cat doesn't say anything more, and his silence suggests to her that it is a confession rather than resolved opinion. She does wonder what he does with these thoughts. She suspects that he will harbor this one and continue to wrestle the stone within him that weighs heavily on each phase of his life and sources new manifestations of self-doubt at each turn. Anna doesn't think like this. It isn't so much confidence or youth that makes her unable to relate to Cat's words, it is something more basic in her. Anna believes that personal experience has inherent value. She sees Elsie work in the garden, and that makes her a gardener. She wonders at Cat's struggle to reconcile the value of his life with some external and subjective idea of success. This is not the criterion Anna uses to grade someone's identity or, more importantly, heart. But the value of a life cannot always be settled in economic terms, Cat knows this. So why then does he not recognize it, she wonders? She doesn't argue the point with him but does make sure to express her belief in other words and in other conversations.

Have you come to terms with this feeling of being a fraud?

The highly competent believe that others possess the knowledge or talents to succeed and that they themselves hold only a small fraction of what these others have. That's what I've read.

But if that's the conclusion, what can one do? How does one escape this?

I don't know, but it gives me some solace in terms of how I feel about my own effectiveness. Maybe I became a competent cheesemaker because I fully grasped and acknowledged my limitations. Now that I am a cheesemaker, I am operating in a new context, competing against expectations.

Everything that Cat says makes sense to Anna in a theoretical way, but she does not see how any of this matters enough that he should worry. But she thinks on it and the next day, while standing guard over the pasteurizer running its course in the cheese room, she approaches him again on the subject. This time, alone with Cat, she talks, not as someone from a different generation or as an intern, but as an equal being. It is not at all peculiar in the cheese rooms and caves to find two people talking as if in a therapy session, a confessional, or a philosophy seminar. The solitary, monk-like nature of the work leads anyone who spends enough hours in it to find delving into such matters as normal. While they wait for the air space thermometer to rise to the necessary temperature for pasteurization to begin, she tells him.

I read a little bit about what you were saying yesterday.

Anna smiles. She is excited to label him with the strange sounding term she has discovered, but she continues knowing that it is not so much a diagnosis as something for them to laugh at. The air space thermometer hits the magic number, and he begins writing down the time along with the temperature of the milk, the air, and the recording device. He listens to her as he writes.

Yes?

I think you might be suffering from a little bit of the "imposter syndrome."

Suffering? Imposter?

Once the words sound, their humor echoes in the silence that follows.

Well, maybe that is not the right way to say it.

Anna knows that Cat's moods steep more in the comedy of life than in the tragedies of identity. His chin shifts to the left and his eyes widen fully, releasing the tension around his brow line. His posture signals to Anna that he approves of the term.

No. Maybe you're right… if so, what do I do?

Anna realizes that Cat, one of her ten over the past year, has just switched spots in the circle of characters. He had been something of a fatherly type, more of a teacher really, somewhere in between those two. Now he has become something different, if for just a moment, like an older brother or something close to that. She is starting to understand what he has been talking about. She and Gabe both feel ready, competent even, to start their own life and possibly their own farm. All creation must be done with a bit of zeal and faith.

Something else about the conversation marks a pivotal moment for her. He had granted her the right to have an opinion, and she feels like her convictions are as good as anyone else's. It is the teacher telling the student, you can go now. Just as the temperature had reached the moment that by definition says "pasteurization has now commenced," so too has the voice inside her become fully formed, ready to come out of its mould and stand on its own. It is ready for the aging room.

The principles that guide our discovery of who it is we love should inform all our decisions.

That feels a bit too naïve.

I think any process for making decisions could be questioned on some level.

That's because you're a contrarian... in a good way.

Don't get me wrong, I'm not suggesting that we all know how to discover love in the right way, in a healthy way. But even business decisions here on the farm, for example, are calculated to some degree with that in mind. It keeps us on the right course.

I think that is the Italian part of your nature coming through, not the New Englander talking. I suppose it's about recognizing fate for you. Like when you ran into Darry after not having seen each other since hiking, and he invited you to that dinner in Boston. Claire decided to stay with Jake and left the farm early, granting an opening for you to come here and fulfill your intuitive desire to make hay. All events in retrospect resemble some storyline of fate, but it's simply our individual stories being walked.

I never suggested at all the notion of fate. I don't spend much time thinking about that. I do believe that life can suggest things to you, sometimes again and again, but you have the choice to make with it what you see fit. I was simply paying attention, listening, each time I found you. You could have walked in the other direction that day in the woods, but you chose to pay attention to what life was presenting to you instead. These opportunities arise every day, and there will be infinitely more as we grow older. We cannot integrate all of it into ourselves. We must stay attuned to those things that will further our dreams and our being. The danger is that, as we grow older, we might stop making decisions that are based in love and passion. The young possess unadulterated minds, free of the hardened prejudices and convictions of reason that don't allow for new ideas. I hope that even when I'm forty, fifty, sixty years old, I will not have lost this freedom as I decide what to do with my time.

But we can't escape our identities being solidified. Some decisions, like marriage or having children, become permanent factors in how we approach new ideas.

Yes. I just don't think those things should preclude new expressions of identity.

What about Cat and Elsie? Do you think they will farm and make cheese forever, until they are too old?

I know what Jake or Darry would say. It's a business like any other, an asset.

So what does that mean? What do you say?

They are both forty-five years old and have done this since they were twenty-three. It is so much a part of who they are that, if they did sell their business, they might get stuck in a state of nostalgia about this life. Wherever they went next would be such a stark contrast that it might be difficult for them even to remember the reality of their former life. It might feel more and more like a dream that had been within their grasp. They might almost forget that they willingly had let go of it, and for what?

Really? I met some farmers before you came here, well ex-farmers, who had started a new life and never looked back. They seemed altogether happy with their decision to stop farming.

I don't doubt that. But Cat and Elsie, they aren't just farming. For them it's something more, and they are equally invested in it. They created it from nothing and grew it to this state. And there is something about making artisanal cheese. I don't know, maybe most farming these days is tied up in something bigger than just the physical labors involved in making sustenance for others. There must be, considering all the young, well-educated individuals out there aiming their sights at all corners of rural America. For Cat and Elsie, after all this time, I think it would be hard to walk away. The choice would be at least bordering on the immensity of having children.

What if they farmed in a different way, somewhere else, somewhere smaller?

Sure. But...

Yeah, I know what you're going to say. The memory of this successful, let's call it creation of theirs will live on the surface of their thoughts every day. I think you're right. Most ex-farmers are not ex-farmers because they want to be. Their businesses die for whatever reason, like someone having a health issue. They need to walk away. Cat and Elsie are living within a vibrant, healthy ecosystem that sustains them financially, spiritually, and in their relationship. How could they leave, no matter what someone was offering them?

Exactly. But who knows? We are not them and cannot know what it's like to be them.

Anna and Gabe have taken many walks around the dirt roads that stretch for miles in every direction from Elsie and Cat's farm. During this last week of their internship, they walk two or three times a day and talk without so much as a breath or pause. The state of flux during this transition compels them to talk through every scenario. Every angle of what is, was, or could be. All of the past, present, and future is under scrutiny. They have found that walking sets a calmness to their discussions. No longer guided in their meanderings by a destination, Anna and Gabe now are climbing to something they will have to invent. Their ideas are transforming into dreams on these open roads.

Whatever it is that they have learned from Elsie, Cat, the goats, or making cheese, they will not comprehend fully what it means in their own stories until years from now. They have stayed long enough to get a sense about what it means to dairy and live that schedule. Milking morning and night. The urgency of the work of making cheese and taking care of each batch. Those daily routines must be accomplished, no matter what day of the week or what holiday has come. But they also have been there briefly enough so as not to become used to working for someone else. They still are willing to take the risks necessary to work for themselves. They have found a companionship in the way they work together, live together, and ponder their own lives together. Watching each other work physically outdoors or delicately within the cave has heightened the growing attraction between them. Their work ethic, their speed, their thoughtfulness, and the positive nature which they bring to their tasks all contribute to deepening their affections for one another. In the end, they find themselves acting with that charitable nature offered only to a lover. They have achieved a perfect blend of equanimity and fire, a result so unexpected and unique, and every future decision will pass through this dynamic between them. They can now rely on their intuition, without apprehension. Whatever is to be derived from that mainstay, they will have molded together.

The road leads them once again to where they had started, the farm. They put their conversation on pause as Anna heads straight for the barn to start milking. Gabe goes to the pasture to bring in the goats and discovers that they are in their usual spot on the edge of the woods, underneath a large oak tree. For some extraordinary reason, they have decided never to chew the bark off it. Maybe they wanted to ensure the health and long life of this tree and thus the shade it offered them. At this spot, they receive the cool breezes that sweep across the open fields of the valley floor, sending flies and mosquitoes out of their purview and giving respite from the heat, which they seem more than any other livestock animal to loathe. Their favorite meal is right at hand in the prickly bushes and young trees; a feast they will choose any day over just plain grasses. Gabe goes to this spot to call them forward, but the weather is just too perfectly matched with their full bellies. The goats don't budge. A rare sight for sure, but it does happen every so often. They choose to be goats, not livestock. He feels bad disrupting the obvious bliss that they have all agreed to inhabit as long as possible, but he must employ them to their jobs. He circles the great oak tree. No grass surrounds it, not from the nibbling of goats but from their sprawling in repose beneath it so many times. Grass cannot grow anymore in this wonderful soft dirt, almost like sand. Not even one goat dropping is within twenty yards of this spot. As he makes his way one last time around the tree, he notices a small sculpture of twig and leaf and wildflowers. Out of the way of where the goats lay about but close enough that he cannot believe it hasn't been destroyed by them. Goats leave nothing unexplored. He decides maybe they had left Anna's sculpture alone the same way they had all collectively decided against eating the oak tree's bark. Or maybe the flowers Anna had lined around it are a natural goat repellent. Did all their curiosity have limits? Whatever the reason, he is glad for it. The power of her sculpture to endure has greater significance, he decides, as he finally rouses the goats and trots with them back to the barn. He can't wait to tell Anna that it is still there.

The Companion

I show up at the doorstep holding a bouquet of flowers, which is only unusual because it is Winter outside. I normally would give flowers to someone only if I grew them myself, but I wanted to give something to Gabe's grandmother. She greets me with absolute generosity and takes the flowers. She is holding, smelling, and beaming at them as she leads me to the kitchen, where she cuts the bottoms and finds a vase. She ushers me into the small eating area, the less formal dining room, where she places the flowers at the center of the table. She pulls out a chair and offers for me to sit with the caring nature of an old Italian grandmother: sit, sit, sit. A demand, but one full of love and invitation. The table is set for three, and I can smell everything Gabe had told me about her cooking.

Gabe just went out to the garden for a minute. He's checking on something for me. Ever since his grandfather died, I cannot seem to manage the garden by myself.

I turn and look through the window behind me. I see a garden altogether different from the one Elsie tended. A branching stone pathway meanders amongst an array of non-native plantings, stone walls and streaming fountains. All orchestrated and deliberate. This is something born out of the imagination. It seems as if it belongs in a landscape design book, its unique characteristics and architectural qualities deserving a place with the English style, French, or Japanese. Gabe turns a corner, strides along one of the paths, and again appears to me in a new light. I remember the young woman in the woods who first spotted the slipshod Gabe with his red bandana. Now I sit here peering out of his grandmother's window, watching him wander in the garden. The garden built by his grandfather, after whom Gabe had run out of the woods, hoping to see him one last time before he died. It occurs to me that Gabe, whether in the woods or the city, at the farm or his grandparents' home, maintains a constant character that seems unaffected by context.

The summer before his grandfather died, Gabe came up here every morning and worked in the garden, tending to everything, since his Nonno could not. He was very sick with the cancer, you know, even though he wouldn't show it.

What's that part over there?

Oh, that's my garden.

What's in it?

Nothing right now. I grow tomatoes, snap peas, salvia, and thyme. But mostly tomatoes. For eating, not canning. We buy in those to make our sauce.

You make your own sauce? I've always wanted to learn to do that.

Well, Gabe can show you how. He helped us and learned the whole process that summer he helped Nonno. We made over a hundred and fifty jars that year. We give away a lot of it to family.

I wish I could see it with all of your plants growing in there. It looks like the perfect size.

Yes. But the light isn't so good there. See that wall there? It shades my tomatoes too much during the summer. We tried other spots, but that was the best we could do. Oh well.

Gabe enters from the garden and sees me sitting by his grandmother and talking. I turn to meet his gaze. He says my name, and I don't hesitate for a moment. I stand up and hug him. Despite having just met his grandmother and her watching, I experience an overwhelming sense of familiarity in hugging him. His grandmother looks on approvingly and smiles like she is an old version of myself, bearing witness to her younger affections. She reaches out and puts her hands on us, one on each of our shoulders, not to tear us apart, but to share in our embrace. Or maybe to bless it. She smiles and lets out an almost giddy laugh as she directs us to sit, sit, and have some lunch. It is ready. After having put us in our seats, she comes in and out of the room from the kitchen four or five times, carrying plate after plate.

I so rarely get to cook for others anymore. I am so excited to eat. My appetite is always strongest when I get to cook for someone.

Every day, she cooked lunches like this for Nonno and me, after we were done working in the garden. That was actually why I did all that work. It was completely worth it.

His grandmother receives the compliment and smiles. She continues to move around, getting up and bringing in another course for us to eat. All homemade. The pasta rolled out the night before, dried, and cooked today.

Don't worry about me. Eat, mangia, mangia.

The small round table with its cushioned chairs. The room full of warm smells and the sounds of clinking plates. The infectious smiles and laughter of Gabe's grandmother as she finally comes to a rest and sits. All of it feels to be some sort of celebration. She asks us questions about the future, but not to guide us or make an opinion about our plans. Her motivation to know our plans is solely to know, like the way one reads a good book. She wants to imagine our story together. She listens as approvingly as one ever could, giving us the right to do whatever we desire.

Oh, to be young.

She says this at least three times that day. With the sign of the cross and sending a kiss from her fingers up to the heaven, she also repeats:

If your grandfather was still here…

As his grandmother stretches us to what the future holds, Gabe pulls the conversation back to times long past, to stories about when she was setting off into the world with his grandfather. Some he has heard and others he has not. She finally capitulates, and we venture downstairs to a room hung full of black and white photographs. His grandmother walks up and down the walls, looking at her young face, those of her sisters and cousins and all their young husbands, wives, boyfriends, girlfriends. Sometimes she must reach far into her memory to distinguish a figure, until she decides, oh yes, that is so and so. All the photos show youthful, well-dressed, smiling young adults. They are twenty-somethings but seem older and wiser in their eyes than anyone in my own generation. They laugh and joke with each other in the photos with a certain rebelliousness that is in stark contrast to their own parents and grandparents. At the same time, they seem… more prudent. That is the best word I can find.

This is you and Nonno, Right?

Yes, yes that is us right before we got engaged.

I love this picture. Can I get a copy of it?

In the picture, Gabe's grandfather is dressed in a suit, and his grandmother is in a white daytime dress. The scene is casual, yet their elegance speaks to how socializing is held as a privilege for their generation. He is reaching for her in a loving and spontaneous way. She laughs and seems surprised that he would be so affectionate in front of the camera. Their hug is a kind of playful wrestle between young lovers, so rarely seen in old photos. It is the only such photo in the entire room. Her mouth is open wide in laughter. I can hear her laugh in the photo. His grandfather's gaze is so set on her, his lips so clearly caught between smiling and getting ready to kiss her. I can see everything between them leading up to the seconds before the shot and can see them kissing long after.

I love this picture. Can I get a copy of it?

I don't know how to do that. I would hate to lose this photo.

I'll just take a photo of the photo right now, is that okay?

Of course. Oh, that reminds me, thank you, I have been meaning to give you something. Your Nonno wrote something for all his grandchildren. Let me go get it before I forget again.

What is it?

It's his legacy.

What do you mean?

His story.

His grandmother hands him the pages. Around fifty of them, all written on an old typewriter.

He didn't finish but did manage to get a lot of it done. Here, take it, take it.

Gabe reads the title page and then turns it to get a taste of this surprise. The notion of getting to hear his Nonno's voice again, even if only by way of words on paper, brings a palpable excitement to his eyes. In the nonchalant way that his grandmother had handed it to him, I start to understand that it is typical for him to receive things of real worth from his grandparents whenever he visits. This is the last installment of a lifetime of gifts from his Nonno, who had supplied a young Gabe with countless presents for his mind and intellect, not to mention his heart.

After, while his grandmother cleans up from lunch, Gabe turns to me and tells me a story about the summer he took care of his grandfather's garden. One day he was tending to some trees, sculpting the young branches as his grandfather rested on a stone bench. It is a slow and tedious task, as the ladder does not allow for a good approach to these unique trees. For the whole hour of the endeavor, his grandfather sits in the same manner, almost like a statue as he observes Gabe, but with a quality of peace and a liveliness in his eyes.

His watching me was unlike anything I had ever experienced and will never forget. Many years earlier, before he ever got sick, he once showed me with great specificity how to mow his lawn. How to make each turn in order to do the job most efficiently and to avoid shooting grass into any parts of the gardens. Then, he had been watching the job I was doing. This time, he was watching me. He was taking absolute delight in just watching his grandson. He may have been remembering me as a little boy or imagining the man I would become many years from now with my own family. But I would venture to guess that he was just watching me, completely present in that moment and only in that moment. He was observing who I was at that very instant, his twenty-year-old grandson, silently and patiently tending to his garden, while he was too sick to do so. I had chosen to do this as a way to be helpful, with only my grandmother's elaborate lunches as payment. Although I had volunteered in various ways up to that point, I am sure it was my finest hour, as they say. I still imagine him sitting out there, and I can see myself perched on that ladder. The more I think about that summer and that moment in particular, I realize I was truly engaged in living. To appreciate, the way he was, without reservation, past all fears, with total clarity of mind. This total awareness is the triumph of peace. The strange thing is, I never really considered beforehand that it would mean much to me, to my grandmother or grandfather, the tending of his garden. I just casually, naively maybe, decided that it might be something I would do. Now, with each passing year, that decision has become one of the most important things to me. I don't think that anything has or will continue to teach me as much as the moments of that summer, the silent moments shared between a man about to die and a young one about to start a life.

.

abe wears his usual button-down shirt. It is the shirt that
defines him in any moment. The rest of his clothing is less
important to him. Even when we first met on the trail, he wore lightly colored button down shirts more often than a t-shirt. Until this
night I hadn't realized how much his choice of shirt plays a role in his
attempt, knowingly or not, to set himself just a bit on the outskirts
of his milieu. He wears the shirt the same way in all situations, with
the sleeves rolled in usually two but no more than three loose folds.
The collar is left unbuttoned, even with his selection of a tie for the
event, and the shirttail is never tucked in evenly all the way around.
Tonight was no different, despite the fact that the focus for the next
two hours would be on Gabe alone. Him and his work. Gabe had
told me that one of his professor's first bit of advice to the graduating
art majors was to dress nicely. No one wants to buy art from a loser.
The professor had paced before the students and come to a stop in
front of Gabe. Just wear a nice purple shirt, the professor said, smiling and smoothing the fabric at Gabe's shoulder with the demeanor
of an old Italian man. Tonight, at first glance, Gabe's shirt is blue
with thin vertical stripes. A blue that tends in the direction of a warm
ultramarine with a hint of magenta and leads the discerning eye to
decide, in the end, that it is in fact purple after all.

You should try the cheeses. They are from the farm that Anna
and I worked at this past winter.

Really?

People seem more animated by the story behind the cheese plate
than with Gabe's work. It is not necessarily because of the work itself,
but because the subject of food is more accessible. While Gabe sends
off a small group of finely dressed people to taste the array of fresh,

semi-soft, and hard cheeses, I observe an older woman taking her time at each of Gabe's pieces. She doesn't take notice of others and almost bumps into a man holding a glass of white wine as she shifts from one work to the next. He looks perturbed as she fails to excuse herself and aims her attention immediately at another of Gabe's paintings. The man shakes his head at her and scurries off in another direction.

I go over to the plates of cheese that I helped to prepare and place a good quantity of the white mold-ripened cheese on a cracker with much of the pillowy rind still attached.

Oh, you can eat that part?

Yes.

Is that true with this one too?

Yes. But most people don't with the hard cheeses. With the younger white mold cheeses, it is more common.

So you must be one of the cheese makers?

I did make cheese for a while, but not anymore.

What do you do now?

Normally, I would respond that I am still figuring it out. But for some reason unknown to me, I react to this question in an unusual and visceral way. So often this question is used to decipher an individual's worth. I find these exchanges reductive but even find myself posing the question when socializing, knowing that others want me to ask it of them. Tonight, some part of me would rather the question be, 'what are your interests?' or even 'what is your focus?' And so, I respond as if that had been the question.

I am a bit of a sculptor. I work mostly with natural materials.

Really? Where can I find your work?

I realize that my attempt at a more elevated trajectory has failed and consider how best to end the conversation immediately. The woman reads my pause and understands it would be better to end the conversation too. She tells me that she needs to go say hello to someone on the other side of the room. I go to Gabe.

Do you like these things?

No.

Then why are you showing your work?

Isn't that what you have to do?

I realize in that short exchange how serious Gabe is and how his seriousness enables his thoughts and dreams to become a reality. I recall stacks of organized work that he has produced in his short career as an artist. Something in him propels him forward. Despite his lack of belief in himself, he creates and then displays it for the world to see. What distinguishes him from so many other young twenty-three-year-olds? How is it that he can take his vision and apply it to his life in such a tangible way? Mould himself. Mould the world around him.

It is difficult to make something that only a very small group within an already niche group will appreciate and, furthermore, appreciate enough to buy it. Even the cheese on display here from Elsie and Cat's farm. Even these cheeses are known and consumed by only a very small group of people.

But at least their cheese could be bought and appreciated by just about anybody.

I frown. Gabe softens his tone.

I know, it can seem pointless. But what I mean is, we have to put ourselves out there. Even the poet who writes for some unborn stranger in the future must contend with this in some way.

So what should I do then?

What do you mean?

You are so good having a vision of things. Once you narrow in on something, it is already underway. You can't stop until you make that thing happen. You had an idea that you wanted to make hay, and you actually did that. You went to the woods to hike and record your journey in these drawings and paintings, and you did that. Even the way you knew exactly what you wanted to get out of college before it even began.

I don't know. I was never fully aware… I didn't really examine myself fully until I met you. I feel like I am still just learning to see myself in the context of the world around me. How I fit into it. How I fit in with others. Especially others. I couldn't really see anybody until you showed them all to me.

That is probably true.

Let's face it, I am just more naïve to put myself out here and show the world my work in its infancy. I know my better work is still ahead of me, but I have to start now. I'm sure that the first year Cat made cheese and brought it around to cheese shops and restaurants, it wasn't nearly as fully realized as it is now. There is actually something deeply fascinating about the trials of someone's beginnings. I would rather have interned with you when the farm was in its infancy. To see how things truly were held together with baling twine. To see Cat run around with not enough time even to complete the day's tasks. To see Elsie struggle in making sense of the finances of a fledgling young business. To see them in the act of creation instead of the more finely sculpted vision as it is now. I am that now. Here, peddling my misshapen cheese to strangers, hoping that someone who just loves cheese will see something of worth here. See that my passion has come through enough to qualify it as a legitimate product.

Okay, but you are still the one with the vision.

The truth is Anna, you are the one with more vision. At some point, I know that I will be standing at your art opening and that you will be fully realized, or at least more so than you can imagine now. We probably will hate being there as much as we do now, but you will see in the very near future that you have just as much vision forming the world you want to inhabit. I've seen the way you approach your work, whether it is a sculpture hidden amid the forest floor for no one to ever find or a piece maturing in your studio. I have seen the way you intuitively engage your medium. You have complete control. Not in a sense of being tightly wound, but in a fluid sense. You move about. Your hands touch and shape things in a way that, to an observer like myself, seems one hundred percent intrinsic and without pretense. I, on the other hand, work at least eighty percent of the time trying to realize those types of moments, just trying to get to that state of being free of any self-conscious tendencies that are wrought with forced ideas and false imitations. The only thing that keeps me going is that, if I work long and hard enough, I do get to feel that moment of release from myself. To a place where my hands make strokes that are commanded, not by thought or reason, but by something else undefinable. It is in this brief hour that I lose contact with time. With place. I become what I believe to be a painter. But I was not even aware of any of this until I watched you step into this mindset so naturally, like how sleep comes to us at night. We lie in our beds and, without even trying hard, drift into the unconscious, not knowing how we got there. When you set yourself down in front of a heap of clay or earth, you fall so easily into that other realm of creation. That is why you don't see how much you are guided by vision. The vision you possess is so abundant as to be transparent to you. And besides, you have what matters more than anything. The necessity to do the work, more than merely the will. You will always make things.

The older woman who has been so absorbed in the show reaches the end of the row. She turns her attention away from the illusory world of color and sets her gaze on the live images of people that have been in motion around her this whole time. She is smiling. Content even. As if she had just finished a good book and was letting the ending settle in. She passes our way, towards the food, but doesn't take anything. I watch her as she wanders the room, just looking about as if she has new eyes to see with and everything is interesting to her now. Even the shadows on a white wall seem to have tremendous potential for viewing. The contrasts of light and dark, the subtle change of hue as one color plays off another. A warm touch of light next to a cool white. A soft shadow and a crisp reality. The overall mood of color and illumination matter more than the details. Things are alive and moving.

The woman approaches one of the organizers.

How long will this work be here?

Oh, only tonight actually.

But I thought this was the opening reception?

It is. But this is a one-time event. This isn't an actual gallery even. You see, we try to offer different venues for our artists, spaces that we believe match the artist's work and the interests of the community that we go to.

So you put on this event?

Yes. I helped organize it with the artist, Gabriele. He is working on bringing this same series of work to another venue in another region. That is, what doesn't sell tonight.

I thought the artist was a woman.

No, Gabriele is an Italian male name.

This whole time, as I looked at all the drawings and paintings, I was imagining a woman making them. The brush strokes were decidedly done with the thoughtfulness of a woman, I told myself. Strange, to look back at the work now and realize I was wrong, that these images are the work of a man.

Does it matter?

No. Well, I don't know. I guess it shouldn't matter. But to be honest, I am a bit reassured looking back now, that a man can see the world this way. I think it does matter a bit perhaps. At least for me it does... Is the artist here?

Yes. He is right over there. In fact, this young woman standing next to you is his girlfriend. She could introduce you if you'd like. This is Anna.

The old woman walks over with me to find Gabe by one of his paintings. He stands in front of it, observing the piece like anyone else would there. Most people have left by now, and it does not seem peculiar for him to be looking at his own work on the wall. The cheese plate is almost empty. The wine mostly drunk. Just as I am about to reach him, where he stands fixated on one specific drawing, his attention jerks to the right. The man who earlier had been bumped by the very woman standing beside me now walks brusquely past Gabe with one of the larger paintings from the series spread between two hands. Gabe turns and shyly motions to the man. I can tell Gabe is baffled. They won't be taking the work down for another half hour.

Oh no, this is mine. I bought this first.

Then the man turns his head with his chin tilted up and continues forward in his triumphant gait. Gabe's body turns with the motion of the strange man but doesn't follow him. A startled look of confusion and powerlessness scrolls over his features. And the man disappears. Out of the building. The painting is gone.

Congratulations on your sale.

Oh, Gabe, this woman here would like to meet you. She very much appreciated viewing all of your art.

Gabe stands still frozen from the rude encounter with the well-dressed man who purchased one of his paintings. All of his thoughts about the encounter are right there in his gaze. How strange it is to have someone now possess a part of him. To carry it off, pull it unknowingly away from the actual creator of that piece. The intimacy he feels with that landscape portrait of his journey through the woods. The care and time he put into making that image come to life. The vulnerability of it all. It was being bought and carried off in the most unexpected way.

But this is what you wanted right? For someone to love it enough to pay money for it? And with that, you know now that it will have a home, where it will be taken care of and loved. What's the alternative really? This should be a good thing, right? Sure, I wish it had been the old woman who seemed to be captivated by your work all night and wanted so much to meet you and shake your hand. The one who couldn't believe that a young man after all could paint in such a way, in a way that she believed only a woman could. But, in the end, she didn't buy anything. It was that man who did. And we cannot know why, or how it will affect him, or who will encounter it now. You will never know the full story of that painting's life ahead and all the relationships it will have with countless individuals who happen into that man's home. There will be so many things you create that will leave your hands, be out of your view, and continue on with a life of its own, making others feel things, think things. At no point can we ever know the full extent to which all of our creations affect others. It is this knowledge of that potential that propels us to make more, to imagine the next thing, and to pursue ourselves in all of our work.

D on't you worry that things won't work out here in the real
world?

I'm not sure I would define any place or time as more real than
another.

What I mean is, don't you think there was something too make-
believe about forming a relationship while hiking in the woods? It
is not exactly what life will be like anymore, next year or in twenty
years.

Our relationship didn't really begin until we were interns at the
farm actually.

But even there. There is a quality to that experience that reminds
me of college even. And college is certainly not a real world experience.

The farm was nothing like college. College is a sheltered immer-
sion in the world of ideas, considered almost exclusively in the
context of the limited perspectives of your peers. The farm is life in
its most basic terms, sustaining a family with the providing of sustenance to the community. In fact, if I agreed with your premise that
some worlds are more real than others, I would put forth the idea
that a farm is one of the more real places I have ever been.

Regardless, it is a transitional experience for you, one which is
controlled and kept safe from the demands and risks of what I say
is the real world. I just worry that eventually your relationship with
Gabe will not survive in the world of work, which is what your lives
will be from this point on.

I'm not worried about that.

How can you not be even a little hesitant?

Claire and I finish our discussion about relationships as others come to sit at our table. Gabe sits at another table, and Jake joins him there with a group of young people that I remember seeing at various farmers markets last summer. Once everyone has settled in their places with their plates full of food, a woman stands up to give a toast. She is the same age as Gabe and I, short in stature with long brown hair and a smile that commands attention from others. Her eyes are beaming with excitement, and she tells the story about her idea to have a farm dinner party before the season begins. Her purpose is two-fold. First is to showcase some of the very early crops as the centerpiece of the meal, mostly leafy vegetables like lettuce, mesclun, and beet greens. Someone has made a rhubarb dish. Second is to meet and socialize with each other before the real business of the summer is underway. She reflects on how the solitary nature of farming and living in a rural environment with so few young people can make nights like this one even more necessary. To share meals with others. To share conversation. Simply to share each other's company. I agree with most of what she says, but, having left the farm and now looking back, I am almost nostalgic about the amount of time spent alone. Thinking in my head. Daydreaming. It had never seemed too out of balance for me. And besides, Claire had been there, and then Gabe.

The idea of a farm dinner before the growing season seems just novel enough to make all the interns from a good number of the farms in the county gather together. It has a bit of the air of a pep rally before a big high school game. Gabe, Claire and I are the only alumni to partake in the festivities. And Jake is the only outsider. All the others are mostly a new crop, led by a couple of veteran interns who have been working in the area for three or four seasons and are now serving as managers. The speaker had been at this farm for two years and convinced the owners to allow use of one of their fields and their kitchen for the evening.

Obviously there are also plenty of local cheeses and grass-fed meats. A new intern at one of the vegetable farms has been keeping a sourdough culture alive the past two years and made a large heap of gnarled breads. The young woman gives due credit to the origins of the individual foods, bringing to light the names of the women and men who cultivated or produced each ingredient on the tables. As she speaks the names, everyone offers a respectful silence and waits to hear either their own or that of someone they know. When she describes the meat in the chili dish, she talks about a man who had started a new business this past winter about an hour north of here in the city. Kurembera is his name. I am listening casually to her, not particularly attached to those involved. But when she mentions that the man is a refugee from Rwanda, I realize it is the man Gabe and I had met on the trail.

He buys the day-old goat kids from numerous dairies throughout the state, puts them in his minivan, brings them back to his farm, and raises them up for the local markets in his area.

It is a small state and coincidences like this happen more frequently than one would guess. Still, I am amazed at how events seem to coalesce within the circles of my life in a more and more succinct way. My first thought after having exhausted this feeling of predestination is one of wonder. Did Kurembera find himself looking out from that mountainside, seeing a world familiar enough for him that he would decide to create something of his own here? I tell Claire and the others sitting by my side about how Gabe and I met him along the trail.

Are you sure? Maybe that is a common name among the people of Rwanda?

He told us he worked in a market, selling food to other immigrants. I'm certain it is the same person.

Something about the opportunity to share in the food raised by the man I met from the woods makes me feel as if I am sitting at the table as a guest might in a new culture. I would again have to try whatever it was that was given to me. But, unlike the time at Kate's house with the moose stew, I begin to come to new terms with the eating of meat. Being more connected to the process of producing food, I have discovered a new hunger. It does not occur as a contradiction or rejection of my previous vegetarianism. It comes to me without the need to reconcile or rationalize but instead as something within my senses, something more guttural. The knowledge of where and by whom this animal was raised leads me to this transition.

While I dwell in the profundity of this shift within me, the conversation at Gabe's table is a whirlwind of subtle and overt ideas around money, capitalism, and the seemingly romantic visions of young utopians driven to agriculture.

Don't you think it is better to have built a business yourself? I think there is a difference between a farm where an individual or a couple builds their dreams and one where dreams are bought. And trust me, there are plenty of people that just try and purchase them rather than put the love and care into making their dreams come true.

Look at this farm though. It is incredible. Everything is in its place. Of course, there are no animals here, and it is much easier to clean up after vegetables. The barns are almost clean enough to hold catered events. Would you rather buy a farm like this, or some run down place? And who could afford this place but someone with a lot of money?

Yes, but the farmers have been tending to this place for over twenty-five years. I'm sure it didn't look like this when they got started. And I don't think they spent those years working to make a haven like this simply to make it worth more at sale.

You know, there are people from the city with a lot of money who want to own a farm for whatever reason and who look for young farmers to manage and run it for them. I heard about a couple who was offered complete control in starting a business of their own, whatever they wanted to do, on some person's land who didn't know anything about farming.

That seems like a disaster waiting to happen.

Why?

It is naïve to imagine building a business on someone else's land would be worthwhile or fulfilling. Putting money and sweat and infrastructure into someone else's land, not a good idea.

I know of an older couple who must be close to seventy now. I think they should let some young couple come live there and take over for them. It would be perfect.

That too. What makes you think that a young couple is entitled to this older couple's most valuable asset? It's not that easy you know.

Jake is the lone voice advocating for a more pragmatic approach to understanding the realities of financing and ownership, asserting that farming is like any other business venture in any industry.

If you don't have capital or access to it, you can't expect to be successful.

That's why this opportunity with the rich couple seems so appealing.

In the end, you'll have wished it had been yours from the start.

I think maybe the workers should have some stake in the operations they are working for.

What kind of stake?

I don't know, but they are the backbone…

Don't you see though? The people who own and operate this business are assuming all the financial risk, including the liability for the environment, the workers, and all the countless unknown customers. There is a weight that you cannot comprehend until you bear it yourself. They are the real backbone.

So what are we to do?

Everyone's personal situation is different. All I'm saying is, just because you know a lot about farming or cheese making or anything for that matter doesn't mean that you get to own or start a business doing that thing. Knowledge about a subject, a desire to do something, those things are not enough. In fact, it can even hinder you from being successful. Making pragmatic decisions ensures the viability of your business beyond more than a year or two.

What? What are you talking about?

Again, Gabe finds himself between Jake's combative ideas and the idealistic minds of his peers. He tries to steer the conversation away from the sensitive topics of money, privilege, and the capitalistic nature of farms. He has in mind some of the sayings his grandfather used to make, relating the health and nurturing of a business to that of a personal relationship. Gabe had learned from his grandfather that all aspects of business have transferable lessons to other aspects of life. It could be something as simple as understanding that there are trying moments in the beginning of raising up a new business, just as with a small child in the early years. How much one must sacrifice. How no one is prepared. And to some extent, how people must make it up as they go along. If done well, the rewards of sacrifice pay off years later. Gabe seeks to lend his own voice too, one that he feels will resonate with the yearnings and intellectual workings of these young interns.

Something I noticed when working on Elsie and Cat's farm was how there were two ways to solve a problem. This applies to all things in life. There are times when it is important to change realities, and there are times when it is more effective to change perceptions. Sometimes it is a matter of building physical infrastructure or making concrete visual improvements. At other times, we need to remodel our perspective or even adjust that of other people. In my personal life even, sometimes I need to change what it is I am spending my time doing or who I am around. Other times, it is my perspective on all of those things that can alter my state of mind, my sense of happiness. It's a powerful approach.

Gabe continues on for some time, explaining his philosophy. Most of the table remains silent for the gist of it, and then smaller conversations begin to pop up quietly. In the end, only one or two people are really listening to him. Nevertheless, the conversation and the overall mood at the table is something less polemic than minutes ago. Jake was correct to some degree that everyone's situation is different, but simply pointing to the existence of those differences is not constructive. For Gabe, those differences all come with strengths of their own. Each and every one of them. He sees disagreement as an opportunity to learn something and gain some tool that, moving forward, always would be available for use.

Whoever had said it in the beginning was right, Gabe decides for himself. It is better to build a dream than buy it. It also builds character and sets values in one's core, which is something that a purchase cannot achieve. Later, after the dinner is over and we are on the road driving through the night, Gabe tells this all to me. How everyone had been right about their ideas. It seems to me that he found a way to meld all their diverging thoughts into a newly formed theory about the nature of things for himself.

What I have noticed about you is that you always keep yourself just close enough to others to win their confidence and affection and just far enough away so as not to identify fully with them.

I think you do the same thing.

Maybe. But you seem to do it for the sake of it, not always out of instinct. You've made me aware of it in myself. Maybe it is a pattern in my life, but I don't do it consciously.

For her, it was and is the quest of the individual, the artist. Not to find a world to inhabit, but to create a world in which she feels most alive. It is easy to absorb the already defined perimeters of contemporary life and to heed to its laws and culture. For the artist, that is not her world. Hers is just on the other side, the adjacent mountain, on a parallel horizon where the journey is for the sake of definition, of seeking meaning even though meaning is only temporary, as time and age constantly reveal to her that everything will be seen and interpreted newly again and again.

In the woods is perpetual youth.

—Emerson, *Nature*

We set out early in the morning. Early enough to stop in at a diner in the small town of Bangor, the only thing in town that is alive at this early hour. The dozen other people already inside turn and watch us as we enter. Even the waitress stops whatever it is she was doing to get a good long look at us, register that we are not from town, and then assess us based on our physical appearance.

Do we seat ourselves?

We have packed a lunch and snacks, but this is to be our big meal before we set out. While we wait for our "everything" omelets, hash browns, and sausages, we pull out a small book titled A Guide to Hiking in Maine. Although we both already have studied the pages that concern us for this day, we again look over the details of the trails. Having decided days prior that we would ascend the mountain on the shorter, albeit steeper and rockier path, we still want to explore in our heads what surrounds the mountain and all its possibilities. We read the description of our ascent again. It is different than any other path that can be found in Maine. It presents something between a hike and a climb. Most of it is an exposed tract of large boulders that must be scaled one to the next. For hot summer days, the book suggests bringing plenty of water. The weather this early in the morning is a bit chilly. We have prepared to shed clothing as we go, leaving it along the trail if need be, but not too much, since it may be cold once again when we reach the tundra of the mountain's peak.

Are you two hiking Katahdin today?

Yes. We are. Do you know it well?

No. I've never been. I don't like the woods.

She fills our water glasses, asks if we would like some more coffee, and goes off to attend to other customers.

I like her honesty.

This whole town feels pretty honest to me.

There is something about small town diners in the early hours. They seem the safest places one could ever encounter in American life. Most people are still asleep at this hour on a Saturday. Expectations seem aligned with the slow and easy ways that one drinks a cup of coffee, talks to some friends, and watches others do the same throughout the diner. The affordability of the menu and its universal appeal mark this as a true meeting place for all citizens of democracy. We can feel it. Everyone, at some point, will find their way here and enter the present moment while sipping coffee in accordance with the demands of their own religious rites.

Did I ever tell you about the time I went rock climbing with some friends just a couple hours south of here?

No.

It was in college. Actually they weren't even really friends. I knew the girl, Jesse. She was a friend of a friend. We both liked to climb, so we made this plan to go together. Neither of us had a car, but this boy that Jesse had a crush on did. He was as serious as one could be about climbing. His name was Trip. We all met in his dorm on a Saturday morning around six o'clock. When I first met him in his room, he was already bouldering around, right there. He had constructed a fantastical and almost sculptural collage of climbing walls with various pieces of heavy plywood and futons scattered beneath. Every inch of the room was dedicated to climbing. Jesse's eyes dilated seeing him there, packing up his gear.

We set off in his small, green car. Before leaving campus though, he picked up one of his guy friends to come along. We didn't know he was joining us until we pulled up to his dorm. Trip asked Jesse if she would sit in the back so that his friend could have shot gun. That was the first thing that made me wonder about him. Anyhow, the climb was four hours away. It probably should have been five, but Trip drove as fast as possible. Jesse and I sat in the back seat scrunched up against each other between his bags of gear. I thought we were going to die in that car, he was driving so fast. The radio blared too loudly for me even to suggest driving more slowly. And besides, I didn't really know any of these people, especially the boys. Looking back, I wished I had said something. I don't think either Trip or his friend, I can't remember his name, ever said more than a couple of words to us during the whole drive. Jesse was smiling, nevertheless, in anticipation of getting to climb with him. The reason I am emphasizing the details leading up to the climb will become apparent. You see, once we got there, unloaded our stuff and hiked into the rocks, the two boys started right off climbing up without so much as a word about the plan. Trip knew the rocks and went first, scurrying up to set the ropes for all of us to use. Within less than twenty minutes, he was hidden from view, but we heard him calling out things to his buddy every so often.

Why do I feel like this story is not going to end well?

No. It's not that bad. Not the way you think.

Does Trip...?

No. You'll see. It's not that kind of story. So, remember we just drove four hours, hiked in another half hour, and have been staring up listening to these two boys converse with one another for twenty minutes. Finally, his friend calls down to us that we can use the rope and start up. There is no question about it that Jesse goes first. She grabs hold of the rock face that she had been testing with her fingertips while we were waiting. This time, with the firm clasp of intention, she pulls her hips in against the rock's surface, hugging her body to the mountain as if a magnetic field had pulled her there fast to the rock. Jesse's excitement about climbing with Trip is clear to see, but Trip is far above and not looking down. Within less than five other grabs and pulls, Jesse slips and the rope does its job of catching her. In fact, she doesn't fall more than a few inches, but the way she slips jerks her body quickly, and she lets out a brief and sharp scream. I couldn't see when it happened, but her arm had scraped badly against some rock and tore open.

Oh my gosh.

I call up to her, but she doesn't say anything. She isn't far up and quickly comes back down, jumping the last few yards. Before I can even reach out to lend a hand, she pulls an extra shirt from her pack and wraps it around her wound. Are you okay, I ask? No, she says, and won't take the shirt off her arm to show me the cut. It's bleeding too much to show you. Can you call up to Trip and tell them we need to go. Okay, I say, but Trip can't hear me, so I have to relay through his friend. We need to go, now, I say, Jesse is hurt. I watch as he tells Trip. Is it really bad, because Trip wants to keep going just a bit further? Yes, I tell him. Are you sure, he says again? Jesse is just holding her arm, staring off, focused on whatever it was that had happened underneath that shirt. After what feels to be a lengthy conversation between me, this guy and Trip, they finally give in and come down to see what is happening. Let me see, Trip insists. No, I don't want to undress it. It's bleeding too much. Jesse is sitting on a rock at this point almost in tears, which she is holding back only due to her crush on this kid.

Then, out of character, Trip kneels down beside her and talks in a sweeter tone than he has all day. She shows him the wound. I was probably five feet away, but close enough to see all the blood and that dark red flap of torn skin hanging off of her. She holds it out for him, waiting for him to respond. But before he makes up his mind on the severity of the situation, my mind has already decided that it has had enough. I say aloud, slowly and in slurred speech, that I don't feel well. As I start to walk in the other direction, turning my head away from the sight of her arm, I begin to faint. The last thing I remember before passing out is seeing her fold the shirt back over her arm. I wake up with Trip's friend by my side, asking me if I'm alright. I'm fine, having landed on some leaves and earth, but feel a very real pang of regret, the kind that usually comes long after having experienced something and reflecting on it with time and distance. I feel it right there, staring at Trip's friend and then looking over at Trip, who is now packing up his stuff with what I believe to be a tone of condescension and anger at both me and Jesse. I don't want to get back in the car with him, but we have no choice. Jesse is bleeding. We are both reliant on him now for the next four or so hours. In the end, Jesse was fine and never passed out even. She got many stitches. But I will never forget how I felt that day. In Trip's car, remembering him and his friend as they laughed and joked with each other climbing down that rock while Jesse held her arm in silence.

I finish telling Gabe this story. I look at him, and think that perhaps I should have told him a different story, any other story. Why this one, today, as we sip coffee in the tranquil innocence of early morning hours, with all the day ahead of us? I scan my memory and think if there is any other aspect to this story, about Jesse or rock climbing, something else I can add to it. I hadn't told this story aloud since that day, telling a few friends back in my dorm late that night. Something about it is unexpectedly upsetting. I can feel my face warming and my eyes swelling just slightly.

I'm sorry.

Why are you sorry? You didn't do anything. You weren't there.

I know, but someone needs to apologize for guys like that.

The waitress interrupts and asks if we need anything else.

No thank you.

Before we can ask for the check, she places it down on the table and goes over to the other customers. I watch her walk away, glance around the room, and take a look at each of the other groups of people. Then, I turn back to Gabe.

Something about this town feels out of time.

I know what you mean.

I can't quite place it. Maybe, there are places and moments that we aren't meant for, and we find ourselves there by accident. It's not a bad feeling though. It's like being an observer.

Yes, I get that too.

But then, when I look at you, I get a different feeling. Like I have known you my whole life. Or better, I feel like life has a divider dropped down in time. The time before I knew you, and life now.

I agree.

A little more than an hour later, we are walking from our car to the trail head. Having arrived early, we are surprised to learn from the man at the entrance that someone else already has set out before us. We start to understand why Bangor feels the way it does to us, as the wild landscape and mountain rise in front of us. It is always that way, I think to myself, how one must pass through some town on the way to visit with nature. At least here in the Northeast. As outsiders to the town, with our aim at the undisturbed landscape surrounding it, we saw the sleepy main street as humdrum, decent yet unimaginative.

It occurs to us now that the town desires to be so in deference to the sublime that rises and hovers over their collective consciousness. The prosaic routine elapses from view as we are now surrounded by the prolific forest and the sight of an almost alien terrain of rocks leading dramatically upward. Usually the start of any path in the woods is a gradual approach, a few feet wide and often trodden down to a modest brown color with some low grass on each side, a slight incline to indicate that it is time to stretch our legs, warm our muscles to prepare for the later switchbacks and final straight vertical climbs. But here, within minutes, we meet a steep prospect of boulders with only a crisp blue sky atop it. I smile in my surprise, wanting to comment aloud, but only my breath comes out, carrying incantations of amazement. We abandon another usual habit at the sight of this. Those easy walking paths that often start a journey upward, they lend themselves to conversation and almost insist on travelers communicating in some way or another. Light conversations at first, a warm-up for the mind that perhaps leads to the emergence of more significant topics. But with these massive rocks, we must pull ourselves up and over, one after the other. It is difficult to imagine how we might go side by side or in any sort of unison upward. It is clear we will be obliged to a bit of solitude.

Gabe and I begin as best we can, climbing the rocks together, taking turns with who goes first. We cannot make out where we are ultimately headed. Except for the marks painted on the large rocks that guide us, it all looks the same. We realize after just four or five boulders that we will be focused mostly on our footing and our hands as we grab hold of things. We can stop to turn and look about, but we don't do that at all. We climb like young children, perpetually excited with each new challenge. The sun is on our side of the mountain and, with no clouds in the sky, it already paints our bodies with heat. We feel fully engaged in the activity of our climb. We almost race up, but a part of the same team not against one another, as if reaching the summit faster somehow will grant us more pleasure and more reward. The scaling of one hard surface after another is not repetitious at all to us. We pull ourselves over each one with fresh eyes and discover there is novelty in crafting our skills, letting our minds go for the sake of the body. We set aside intellectual memory for muscle memory, transcending to the fluidity of an animal, moving about our terrain as creatures fully in tune with what is below our feet and within our grasp. The seemingly endless façade of the mountain keeps us moving without the need for reflection. We find the right pace despite not knowing the distance we will go. We go on like this until we come across a man, about fifty years old, sitting by one of the enormous boulders, leaning up against it, out of breath and drinking water in deep gulps. We stop.

Hello, we say in unison to him.

He nods his head as he finishes a great swallow and takes a breath.

Hi there… beautiful day, isn't it?

This is what we love about Maine, the stark contrasts the sunlight can make, clean crisp light and shadow. You can see why Winslow Homer painted the way he did.

I'm from northern California. I'm used to light like this.

What are you doing on this side of the country?

I came out here to hike. I'm training, trying to make as many big hikes as I can throughout the country. My goal is to do Mount Kilimanjaro in a year.

Where else have been?

This is the first.

The man's breathing is still fast and loud. He takes more swigs of water and wipes the sweat from his forehead repeatedly as we talk.

He goes on to tell us that he retired early and, after years of sitting at desks, he wanted to get out of city life.

You guys are doing it right, he tells us.

I easily can decipher that he is used to walking on sidewalks, down city streets, on treadmills either in his home or in gymnasiums.

Don't wait until you get old to get to places like this. I wish I hadn't.

His hair has not greyed, and his physique still could be defined as youthful or fit. Despite this, he stands here now, panting against a rock as if oxygen were a foreign gas for his lungs to absorb. He doesn't say much else, and it is clear that he wants us to go ahead of him. He wants to be alone in his training. Maybe he came to the farthest mountain from his home to feel anonymous as he stretches himself out upon this new task, this enterprise of his to be ready for Kilimanjaro.

We leave him there and continue upward, but our rhythm and melody having been interrupted, we find a new pace for our climbing. We find it easier to talk, and we discuss the man once he is out of hearing distance. We had no conscious intention of trying to catch up with the one person ahead of us, but the approach had urged us to move swiftly up the mountain and led us to pass him. Now, mindful that the mountain had compelled us to clear the way between ourselves and the summit, we go at it with more of a meandering course. We stop for brief three-second intervals every couple minutes to look out behind us or down at the steep incline. We feel the heat and sweat just as much as the man at the rock, wiping away the salty water from our eyes with the backs of our hands.

I find it interesting how, a stranger and a brief conversation can change the trajectory of our thoughts and conversation so much. How way leads on to way.

What in particular makes you say that?

I am now more aware of my body. And the peak of our bodies is now. Whatever it is we do, we are so capable now. We moved up those rocks with ease and speed.

The more we talk, the more we find that our thoughts are almost one. Our minds find their way to these similar conclusions upon the same pathways. We voice them aloud, and in doing so, we realize that either one of us could have spoken the other's thoughts. Who was it that just said that? Was it me or him? Is his story mine? And mine his? The voice between two people is often a meeting place for the invisible part of ourselves. We pull out of our minds to mingle our ideas with another's, and we connect there, in the ether, the molecules, the space between our bodies. But somehow, his thoughts and my thoughts had found a way inside one another as if our cell walls were permeable to trust and allowed light upon that sacred map of our inner being. Whatever it was, our voices blended together to one voice, still full of their own convictions and individuality, but resonating from twin minds set upon the same course.

Don't you find that, at different points in our lives, we set out with some singular purpose that occupies all of our thoughts and passions? All our actions through each day arise within the structure of this theme. I mean, how did that man come to the realization that he would train himself with the ultimate goal of hiking Kilimanjaro? For the next year or more, I don't know how long, it will be his focus. What led him to decide that?

Most of us are not so singularly minded.

Maybe not. I don't know. Everyone might actually be like him, harboring some inner guiding thought, consciously or not, a secret to others or even to one's self. Is there anything like that for you, do you think?

I don't know. Probably. I live with some overall questions more than purposes. I'm not sure what to call it. There has been one question in particular that I live with, something unanswerable.

What is it?

It is something I feel completely torn about. It sounds strange, but it is something that I think about... whether it is better to be a great character of a story or the one telling that story.

It's the Homer-Achilles question. Is Homer great because of the story Achilles provides? Or is Achilles great only in Homer's telling of the story?

I don't think I can choose. It feels impossible. The cause and effect nature of their relationship seems unresolvable.

They are distinct, yet one. There is another important individual you're missing. It's more a trifecta than a couple. What about the one hearing the story, the listener, the Horatio, the readers. Neither Homer nor Achilles has any virtue without the listener. It is not until their story is heard that they come into existence.

We are all that. Each of us share in that. Do you think the character is self-conscious enough to consider making such a choice? Isn't it the nature of the characters to be unaware; once they are aware they begin the process of reflection and eventual storytelling?

Everyone's self-conscious, even the protagonist, especially the protagonist more often than not. But what I mean is, do I focus on building the physical world around me, creating a universe inhabited with real people, all with their own "singular purposes" as you say, or do I make it my aim to pay attention to the world and find a voice and the tools necessary to explain what it is that I see, and influence the world by way of words, paintings, something?

But why can't you do both? I'm sure there are plenty of creative people who have it in them to find a balance.

Maybe. But if I had to choose one... that is my dilemma.

This might be taking things too seriously, have you ever considered that?

I know. It's been that way with me since as far back as I can remember. But I plan on taking life less and less seriously as I grow older.

I still think you are looking at it as black or white. For me, life is the entirety of it all, requires all of it. Just as Homer and Achilles are inextricably tied together, so is everything that the soul needs. The human condition requires this I think. Or, to put it more clearly, it is the nature of the human condition to live in the illusion of duality yet seek unity. You need to look holistically at it. The author will get back or hip trouble sitting all day with pens and books and screens. The builder of dreams, the orchestrator of community, she will suffocate without some quiet place to be with her reflections. And all of us need to be the listener, the ones reading the world like we are doing here and now, on this mountain. We come here to listen to what this place has to say. There is a story, countless stories along this path of rocks, dreamt and created by others. Ancient cities are filled with competing tales of different centuries, all made by men and women from the past, but constantly being born back to us now. Nature though tells another kind of story, one woven together not by human beings, except maybe in these maintained trails. There are histories to be read here in the fallen trees, decaying matter, and eroding stream beds, but it is the present that reigns here, a new flower. Whatever it looked like here two hundred years ago or two thousand years ago, the vegetation and its arrangement on these surfaces of rock and ground, that is lost to us today. If these ancient trees could talk we might know, but they serve only as a silent testament to the past. The past is hidden from us here. It's not important. Sure, the geologist in me would consider these rocks and their formation and reach some conclusion through scientific method. Despite the part of me that marvels at what it must have looked like then, these rocks are here only for us to see them in their present condition, for us to grab, hold onto as we pull ourselves further along, up to the top on the mountain. If you want to grab the past, that is in the manmade structures of towns and cities. The story here, it is present to those along the trail and gone when they leave. That man back there carries with him a story, and we walk with ours. We live it, tell it, and listen for it all the same. We leave no memories here, written along this path. Just as with a swimmer in the ocean riding a wave, nothing recorded there, there is no permanency. She disappears under the water just before another wave crashes hard against her and then enters into a fresh new scene, a crisp moment with no allusion to the past or the future. The swimmer rides her wave in a singular event that is hers alone and then is gone, swept back into the currents below. She swims back out to experience it again and again, and we climb the next set of rocks, unaware of the wave's origin or the rock's, but wholly alive with them in their present state here and now.

After some time of talk, there is a period of silence as we climb.

My breath fills my ears such that I lose track of all other sounds, including those of Gabe's movements. I get far ahead of him and don't realize this until I stop for a moment to look out behind me. I cannot see him at all and, in a small panic, I call out his name, "Gabe?" I say it softly at first, and I get no response. I look carefully at all the different boulders, waiting to see a hand or a head of hair poking up from below. I wait. And listen. For some sound to signify where he is. Nothing. I call out again, this time louder, and reach a real sense of panic upon yelling his name the fourth time. Finally, I see his elbow and then his head. He pulls himself up, and I can see all of him. He doesn't see me. He hadn't heard me calling out. He continues upward, slowly gaining on me. I watch him, with my worry echoing to myself alone. I wait for him to catch up with me. I don't say anything about it. I kiss him. But not long, as the sweat on our faces starts to mingle where our lips meet. He kisses me next. But this time I don't let it bother me that we are out of breath and sweating. Unknown to me at the time of our first kissing, many months ago, there was a burning desire within Gabe, something he had kept under lock and key with some insurmountable will power. He held it back from me as well as the rest of the world. So much so that its release was at first a complete surprise to me. An old notion must have been laid in his core being long ago, handed down to him from a past generation. It is not uncommon and best described as prudent. But with each new day, it becomes unmistakable that he has set himself free. There is a canyon of desire to fill, a space so immense and uncharted that he will spend a lifetime unleashing affections aimed at me, my heart, my body. Like the photograph of his young grandfather reaching out to kiss his grandmother, with his eyes wide and set on her, their mouths open with laughter and a primal desire for one another, so too does Gabe reach for me now on that side of the mountain, only a few boulders away from the summit.

Why were you hiking alone for all that time when we first met?

I don't know. I think it came to me, like so many of the decisions I've made, by instinct. I have been realizing more and more that I tend to base everything off of my intuition, rather than others' experiences or even my own.

So, is it an emotional response to things that happen to you? Like your grandfather being sick or having broken up with a previous love?

No. It's not at all an emotional reaction. In fact, I try my best to avoid ever acting upon emotions, the same as I do acting upon reason. I try to narrow my emotions, my fears and hopes, and narrow all the analytical thoughts I can—that is, all the noise of life—and push all of that aside. I then listen, without attachment to any of those sounds, and hear what life is trying to tell me. Then, somewhere inside me, I know what to do.

What about me? Is that how we came together?

I hope so. I think it was.

So we all choose the nature of our lives?

If we build our lives upon a foundation of rational thought, then the continuity depends on it. The same for emotions alone. Everything is held up by our affections and desires. But if our lives are rooted in intuition, if that is the scaffolding that we use to make our lives, then whatever we create is something more true to who we are.

Or, in more basic terms—timing is everything. I think life is simply recognizing. That in every hour or year, we see this or that. We become aware of how time plays just as big of a role in our life as the spaces we inhabit. Inhabiting those minutes there.

The transition is as stark as the sunlight in Maine when we crest over the last boulders and see the plateau of vegetation that is like no other in all the Northeast, stretching for a few hundred yards before us. A strange, unfamiliar shelf of green life, so low to the ground as if sheep had grazed it. But no, it is this way, a fragile and foreign kind of life up here. We walk out along the trodden path of light brown soil that meanders through this wondrous plane of plants and grasses. Our legs feel funny moving so easily along the perfectly level ground after having climbed vertically for so long. The peculiar meadow atop Katahdin is the first of many dramatic scenes, and we follow through its design with absolute curiosity. For some reason, the land below our feet feels to be of another planet, and we walk with the trepidation that such a place commands. Why do we walk anywhere assuming otherwise? Is the world, the earth, that familiar to us already? Do we know its plants, its birds, its insects, the microbial life teeming in the dirt below our feet and in the recesses of a pinhole of that pebble there... do we know it all so well? But this landscape here today, in this light, is like no other, and the organisms here have never before met the organisms on my skin or within my gut. It is their first meeting. I proceed and eventually we begin to jog and then run along that pathway, like discoverers of an indefinite land. It feels improbable to run atop a mountain at full speed with no recourse or cause of injury.

We make our way to the end and see the second stage to Katahdin's peak, a sculptural arrangement of mountain stone. Not exactly like the boulders we climbed to get here, but a creation of sorts, almost architectural, with chairs perched almost on the edge of the mountain, some more dramatic and precarious than others. We sit in different places, staring off in that direction and then another. The views are spectacular and feel more wild and daunting than anything previously encountered along the ridgelines of the northeast.

Some of these rock chairs let you lounge right off the precipice but are hard to reach safely. We are certain that others had made that choice to go and sit in these places, risking everything just for a chance to be in such a scene. We only imagined ourselves sitting out there, deciding that, at a certain point, it is possible to miss the point in trying to connect so closely with the sublime. We draw a line, not pushing to the extreme. I find my farthest reach and set myself there, while Gabe finds his. We sit with devotion for this place and this hour, no longer foreign organisms to this terrain.

The next part, adjacent to the solid rock peak, is an unusual deposit of loose stone, no more than two feet wide, making a path to the other side of the mountain. Embankments of loose stone stretch far below on each side of the walkway. The map in our book refers to this as the "knife's edge" due to the nature of walking along it, balancing on a razor thin path with steep falls on either side. Nothing at all to stop a long fall to the bottom. No limbs or brush or small trees to grab. We start cautiously out onto the path, with no stated intention. It is just a small, unplanned exploration of sorts. I go first, but after less than thirty feet we quickly decide this is not something we need to cross. We had planned to return down the way we came, so it isn't necessary to reach the trail on the other side for our descent.

That trail is more of a typical hike in mountains here, a tree-lined snaking and undulating path. No. We stop. Look about to really get a feel for this too before retreating back to the safety of the rocky meadow. But on our way back, this time with Gabe ahead of me, I stop for a moment as something catches my eye. It is almost nothing, a marking on a stone. The color is something nature might produce, but the marks themselves seem more human in their perfect symmetry, and are something not found in the patterns of nature. It is something so subtle that in retrospect seems impossible to have been noticed. I kneel down and take one minor step off of the trail. Gabe hears my footing produce an unusual sound and turns around to see what it is. He is hyper-vigilant about our safety, especially mine, and questions what I am doing. I tell him that I see something unusual. It seems like a marker for something maybe underneath it. He voices his concern and says it is probably nothing, that I probably shouldn't go off the "knife's edge." I tell him that I'm not going any further, that I can reach it from where I am. I crouch down and lean over the edge to uncover whatever is there. Gabe backs up to get near enough in case I needed a rescue, but such an effort would be futile. I know I am safe; there is a big rock jutting out of the mountain and I can feel it is connected like a stair bolted or welded to the inner structure of the mountain. If there is something here, whoever put it there chose this spot because of this solid flat rock which makes it possible to get down upon the edge safely. I get a hold of the marked stone. I try to lift it, but it too is connected to the mountain and not one of the loose stones. I look closer at it and see that the markings are initials. An inscription of two letters: AT. I try the other stones next to it, one by one, all of them are loose. Gabe attempts to usher me along, worried about my hovering over the edge. He doesn't pester me; it is more of an affectionate concern. It is endearing to know he is worried but not so much as to make the situation more dangerous.

I see something.

A foot long cylinder made of stainless steel, maybe an inch in diameter. One end is sealed, smooth and round, while the other has a coupling threaded into it and capped. I pull it from the stones and hold it in my hand, observing the pipe and marveling at the peculiarity of finding such a thing in this place.

Come on. Let's go.

We go back to the safety of the smooth expanse and find one of the friendlier rock chairs to sit on and investigate this found oddity.

What is AT?

Appalachian trail?

Probably.

I try and twist the threaded end, just because I have to try. No use. I am inclined to leave anything I ever find atop a mountain, unless it is trash, but there is something about this pipe that I can't disregard. When I turn it to the sky and then back down, I can hear something inside

It could be something intended only for the person who is stationed here, watching over this peak and trail. That's probably why it says AT.

Why would they put it out there at such a dangerous place? If that was the case, then it would be in this area, hidden behind one of these boulders.

Once our imaginations settle and enough time passes, I tuck the pipe into my pack, but upon doing so a feeling of unease passes over me. Unsure if I should take such a thing, I leave it in my pack for now but tell myself that I may reconsider before we leave. I turn my attention back to the unparalleled views and the solitude we have found together. The cloudless sky and clean light shines the world at us in a clear perspective. The day is so calm and gentle, it is difficult to remember that nature, or life, can ever be cruel or anything but this. We have caught up with peace this day and have full access to its presence, surrounded by it from all points north, south, east and west. It signals to us a kind of order to everything, a release from the relative nature to life below. An absolute of a kind is here. As we have transcended to this pinnacle from all of our seeking and wondering in the woods, above the other distant mountain tops, I have reached an awareness that is beyond words or specific thoughts, an understanding. Unknown to either of us at the time, this epiphanic feeling is not a one-time event but one that we would encounter on other occasions as we grow older. Having recognized it now for the first time and remaining open to it thereafter, it would become familiar despite its irregular visitations. Perhaps what would come next was actually the cause of our discovery, what forged this quiet and striking feeling in our minds. Or did we come to it before he appeared in the distance, emerging off the boulders and onto the grassy tundra? The events of time play tricks on our memories and all of it now is linked inseparably to the man approaching us along Katahdin's peak.

We watch as the contours of the tall, lean figure focus to a definitive line. The impressions of color and markings about his face are as if made by the artist's palette knife, swaths of paint next to one another, building a textured forehead, the wrinkles of an aged face, and the hue of an old man, despite his full head of hair. It isn't the man we had met gasping for breath along the trail. This is someone else, someone only thirty minutes behind us, who must have made great time up that steep incline of boulders. Where did he come from? We hadn't seen him during any part of our ascent.

His appearance, to me, reflects something about his character. He seems to be an individual worthy of lengthy and contradictory descriptions. His build communicates rugged strength and fortitude, but he moves with a graceful sophistication. I have heard it suggested that each of us has an essential age, the age of our internal dialogue, that we carry from the start and persists throughout our lives. It may be the conversation of a ten-year-old, eighteen, even forty. When our physical age aligns with our essential age, we are at our peak, at the greatest command of our world. The old man only yards away from us is truly exceptional. He has reached his peak at the age of eighty. Despite the difference of several generations in our ages, I feel a strange attraction to him. Does he remind me of what I imagine Gabe will be like sixty years from now? Is it his rare expression of manhood? Is it the look in his eyes that signals all of this to me? Or do all people, having reached that peak within themselves, that grand unifying moment of body, mind and spirit, possess this attractiveness? It may be all of these things and more, but unknown to me just yet is the real reason I am drawn to his character. His story and mine are about to overlap. I am about to discover, or better, am about to be granted an extraordinary convergence, one that two strangers may experience and afterwards depart with a memory of the sacred. We may spend half a lifetime knowing someone and scrape together only a handful of moments where something of serious significance occurs. And then one day we meet some person for a brief hour who carves a large swath into the core of our most cherished records, the ones we turn to in defining our view of the world and the expectations of the life we aim to live. It could be the man swimming beside me amid turbulent waves, whose hand clenches mine and relieves that unbearable fear as he pulls me out of the riptide and into shore. Or the woman on the trail who invites me to her house, feeds me, and becomes my mother for one day of my life. Or the immigrant who reveals to me the nature of where I live. Such moments may mean little to the other but affect us deeply.

The old man sits a few boulders away from us. I can't take my eyes off of him. I watch his every movement. The way his arms move about, the turn of his head as he looks in the direction of the late morning light, his lifting himself on both hands to reposition himself on the boulder. He spends his first moments with his gaze affixed to a single point in the distance, without so much as a hint of interest in the rest of the 359 degrees of view around him. No drink of water, not even a quick swig. He doesn't reach in his pack for a snack or treat, neither pragmatic nor celebratory. Gabe also is looking the man's way in fascination.

He doesn't look tired at all. Look, you can tell his body is completely still. His breathing must be so calm.

From our vantage point twenty yards away, we can see the taut calf muscles and his chosen posture, one that conveys youth. With the same power that the old man uses to focus out there, I keep my eyes on him. Finally, he reaches to his pack and pulls out a notepad. The pages rip about in the air. He secures a page with his hand and forearm and begins to write. After the first two sentences, which he appears to write with the stride of a sprinter, he stops to look again at the point in the distance. Then, only seconds later, he is back again scribbling away at the pad in what must be messy handwriting. He writes as if he is speaking, not thoughtfully crafting ideas into finely dressed phrases. No. He is responding, reacting, discussing, communicating in real time. As if that point in the distance is a beacon sending out messages to him, and he is talking back to it. An anxious longing propels him to write fast and without hesitation, as if the two points have only a brief window of opportunity to talk with one another. He writes for five minutes, but he seems to have written five hundred words on each side of that one piece of paper. He sets his pen down and turns the page over to where he started and reads what he has written one time. He makes no changes to the document and then gently tears the page out of the notepad.

What he does next is what first makes my mind truly wonder. I cannot be certain, time and memory are failing to keep orderly as everything begins to crescendo. He takes the page and rolls it up lengthwise. He stands up and reaches into his pack lying on the rock. What he grabs makes a sound that is distinct to us through the crisp, thin air. The clink is the actual thing that first sets off a wave of goose-bumps up and down the entirety of my body. He pulls out two metal objects, and I can see that one of them is an adjustable wrench and the other a pipe wrench. Two simultaneous chemical reactions burst through my bloodstream. The first one flushes me with an overwhelming dose of dopamine, which to this day I have never felt equaled in any other moment. I am suddenly aware of what seems like a tremendous stroke of fate, so much more than coincidence. Those two things have never before felt so much at odds with one another. The second feeling to course through me is a shock of humiliation, as I know now that I have his possession in my pack. My mind races to quell this second force that is dizzying my senses.

I look to Gabe to see if he had discerned the wrenches in the old man's hands. He hadn't been looking, and I hit at his leg to get his attention. We both look back toward the old man and can see the wrenches in his hand as he walks in our direction towards the Knife's Edge. The sun glints off the stainless steel of a wrench into my eyes. I am sitting with my backpack toward him and see a bit of the pipe poking out of it. I think, if he looks this way, he will see the same flash of light in his eye. As my paranoia heightens, the old man finally looks our way for the first time. The calm and even brighter gleam of his eye reassures me. I wave to him...

I come up here each year to welcome Spring. It was my wife's annual ritual. She passed away five years ago, but I make it my goal to carry on the tradition. I wasn't quite sure if I would make it this year. I just turned eighty.

I don't think I know anyone your age who could do that hike over all those boulders.

I do a lot of walking throughout the year.

We don't talk to the man for a long time. We all remain standing while we meet with our bodies mostly positioned toward the view and turned only slightly to one another. It is not until I show him the cylinder that he changes his bearing. The look that comes over his face has the same sort of vulnerability that I felt, but it progresses quickly to convey a curious sort of delight at this peculiar fortune. It was no accidental find. He looks at me now the same way I had been doing this whole time at him. He sits down on one of the boulders and holds it in his hand. I already feel like I have invaded upon something of his and don't want to pry anymore, but I realize that it is too late. I am already connected to this man now, and I find the one question that I feel would be appropriate to ask.

What does AT stand for? Appalachian Trail?

No. But that does seem likely. It's the initials of my wife's trail name. I would have written all of it, but the stones over there are too small to write anything more than a couple of letters. Avocado Traipse. She had been writing that name since she was your age at trail heads all over the country. I always loved the playful quality to it.

He paused. We give him our attention but let our eyes drift between him and the view. Then he explains it all to us.

I have to admit, there was a part of me that wanted to know someone would eventually find the cylinder. I wouldn't want it to lay undiscovered forever. Even if someone might happen upon it, I thought it would take a certain type to be curious enough to bring it down the mountain and get the tools to open it. You see, when I was your age, I thought that I wanted to be a poet. And I did write, but I had a different career and raised a family. My wife believed in me more than anyone I knew. She encouraged me to write poems. And when I retired about six years ago, I set out to do it despite my age. It took me a while through that transition to even find my voice again, which I felt had been lost to my youth. And then my wife died.

He pauses again, and we keep our eyes on him as he offers us his story. It feels like an unexpected gift.

I returned up here that first Spring alone, to greet the start of a new cycle of life. And as I passed over the boulders to get up here, I had the first line of a poem rattling around my head. I struggled up the mountain, finding the words that came after as I ascended. Reciting each line in my head again and again so as to memorize it. By the time I reached the top I had completed most of it. I copied it out without any edits and placed it under a rock out there on the Knife's Edge. As I walked back, I could hear it flapping about and guessed that, by the time someone else happened by, it would be torn apart or rained on. So the next year, I made this cylinder and brought it up here with that poem and about six others that I was quite happy with. Each year, I bring about a half dozen new ones and write one in my head as I climb.

He takes the cylinder in his hand, puts the wrenches on it and twists until it loosens. He takes the end piece off and puts it in his pocket, then offers me the contents to read...

Somewhere off the trails, in the inscrutable forest, there still may be the evidence of a sculpture or two. But none of them are substantial enough to survive for long, and their location is unknown. Like most of our creations and thoughts and feelings, they are transient and never revealed. Most of our efforts have the longevity of flowers set in the vase, arranged with deliberation and care but with no perpetuity. We disappear, and even the moose meat is all eaten by now. Some of our activities are carried on by someone else, often strangers, like the hay fields that Cat mows every summer. Who cleared those fields originally, de-stoned them, and began the fruitful endeavor of tending to their growth and maintenance year after year? How quickly that creation could be lost if he and Elsie left it to be for even five or six years. Those others are stewards to the memory of creation, like the stranger who keeps one of Gabe's paintings hung. Perhaps the next generations will see something in it too and hang it upon their walls. The endurance of all of these things is unknown, and, although each of us may wonder at whom our distant relations were or what the land looked like one hundred years ago, that is not our concern. We create caves of our own, aging our creations, each moment of our lives, like artisanal cheeses, systematically set in rows and columns, preparing to meet the world and have their moment to nourish us. The old man's cave is that small steel cylinder. His writing secreted from the multitudes but guarded from all those methods of extinction.

Those that do walk by may take note of the flowers in silent arrangement, see the decaying twigs and leaves by a large spruce tree, glance at the painting above the couch, devour within a few seconds a small mouthful of cheese. Or the one who by chance sees the cylinder and opens it, she will interpret it as something else. The field is hers now to tend.